Nee-Jerk Reaction

Also by Ronan Joyce

Week at the Nees'
Hollywood Hoodlums

Nee-Jerk Reaction
VOLUME TWO IN THE MARCUS NEE SERIES

RONAN JOYCE

ISBN-10: 0463623015
ISBN-13: 978-0463623015

For Festus and Eileen.

PROLOGUE

Augsburg-Haunstetten, Germany, 1941

A S THE oversized Mercedes-Benz 770 limousine lumbered toward the air base, the man in the back seat sat uncomfortably in his opulent surroundings. He seldom made a fuss about such matters but the delicacy of the mission at hand underlined the importance of being seen in a vehicle befitting his status in the Third Reich. He eyed the velvet seats and plush carpet and was glad he had cleaned his boots before he climbed inside.

The varnished mahogany panels all around glistened in the sun and he could see his reflection in the polished chrome of the door and window handles. He looked resplendent in his leather Luftwaffe flying suit with the second-class Iron Cross he had won in the Great War hanging below his neck. His closely cropped dark hair, thick bushy eyebrows, and long straight nose blended in nicely with his German face.

He opened the drinks cabinet between the two opposite seats and was surprised to see bottles of the finest Cognacs, brandies, whiskies, schnapps and vodkas. A set of Waterford Crystal glasses, a gift from Joseph Kennedy, the U.S. ambassador to Britain, sat on a shelf of its own lined with velvet padding. Opening a mirrored compartment, he found a box of Upmann's cigars and premium Swiss chocolates. He was relieved to see, amid the unnecessary clutter, a simple bottle of Bavarian still water. Grabbing the bottle, he opened it and poured some of the liquid into one of the crystal glasses. He took a small glass jar out of his briefcase and placed two homeopathic pellets from the jar into the water. Picking up the glass, he placed it to his lips and swallowed the contents, pellets and all.

He had long since taken to consuming his homeopathic remedies in private, such was the vitriolic criticism it prompted from his colleagues. He was horrified that his preoccupation with his health and his unorthodox treatment regimen should be such a bone of contention during his visits to the Berghof.

The road to the air base was lined by squadrons of infantry soldiers who stood to attention and saluted as the car swished past. Even if the size and magnificence of the vehicle had not alerted them to the importance of its occupant, they were forewarned by the red banner that hung from the silver flagpole on the right front wing of the car. It bore a white eagle and swastika inside a black circle—the insignia of the Deputy Führer.

Anxious to hold on to what little power he had left in the Reich, Rudolf Hess took every opportunity to display the trappings of his office. Even if this mission required him to wear a flying suit bearing the rank of a Luftwaffe captain, he was determined to show as few signs as possible of his diminishing status. Over the flying suit, he wore a tunic bearing the insignia of his true rank. He also made sure the uniforms of his staff bore ranks appropriate to their stations.

Erich Sommer, his driver and bodyguard, wore the

uniform of a Luftwaffe major, and Karlheinz Pintsch, his adjutant, wore the uniform of a Luftwaffe colonel. Of course, those were only the ranks they were displaying for this mission; in reality, they were both SS officers of the Gestapo. Both men had been loyal servants since 1933, when Hess had been appointed Deputy Führer, following Hitler's elevation to Reich Chancellor. Until then, they had been career officers in the Prussian Secret Police with special duties to protect government officials. In 1936, when Hitler unified all German police forces into the Gestapo, they became SS officers. Hess had no doubts about their loyalty, despite their rugged and daunting appearance. Their duties often brought them to Hess's private home and they always showed his wife, Ilse, and his son, Wolf, the utmost respect. He knew that both men would lay down their lives for his and that they would protect his family during his absence.

Hess flipped open a mahogany table attached to the door, marvelling at the exquisite craftsmanship and the superior German design. He took a small leather-bound journal out of his briefcase and placed it on the table. The journal was worn with age, but the swastika was still prominent on the front cover. As he shuffled through the book, taking care not to dislodge any of the fragile pages, he considered the names that caught his eye and recounted the events that had brought him to this point in his life. It had been Hess's idea to travel to Britain and negotiate a deal with King George VI to keep Britain out of the war. The Führer had been sceptical at first, but Hess had convinced him that the imminent invasion of Russia would make the prospect of fighting the war on two fronts more likely.

The Deputy Führer had begun formulating the plan six

months before with his friend Albrecht Haushofer, who had been acquainted with Douglas Douglas-Hamilton, the Duke of Hamilton. Hess had arranged to meet Prince George, the Duke of Kent, at Hamilton's estate in Scotland to get him to convince his brother, King George VI, to end Britain's involvement in the war. He believed that the British establishment had no desire to be involved in the conflict in Europe and that their only real concern was the protection of their dominions and territories around the world. Thanks to his conversations with the overbearing Ambassador Kennedy, Hess knew the United States had no intention of entering the war. Through a series of clandestine intermediaries and secret missives, he had reasoned that Britain could never hope to beat the might of Germany, especially with a drunkard like Winston Churchill at the helm. And without the United States, Britain was on its own. After all, the British royal family were themselves of German stock and should have no wish to get in the way of the Nazi desire for *Lebensraum*.

Hess had to admit a certain delight at the thought that his brainchild had the potential to put him back in favour—he had long since been frustrated at being pushed out of Hitler's inner circle by his disagreeable counterparts Hermann Göring and Martin Bormann. The Deputy Führer had always been motivated by his loyalty to Hitler and a desire to be useful to him; however, he had been forced to concede that only through the accumulation of power could he take advantage of his position and keep his place by the Führer's side. But he understood that, should the plan fail, the Führer would deny all knowledge of the mission and dismiss Hess as a madman. This was of great concern to Hess, who was aware there was a chance he would not secure a peace deal and make a triumphant return as a hero of the Third Reich. He had to protect his good name and the good name of his father.

Reaching into the inside pocket of his tunic, Hess removed a letter bearing the official red wax seal of the Führer himself. He opened the letter, which he had received only a few hours before, and read it for the hundredth time. Glancing at the signature written on the bottom of the typed letter, he noted with pride the unmistakable hand of Adolf Hitler. He was convinced the letter, which carried as it did the best wishes of the Führer, would serve as a fitting testament that he was not a madman who disobeyed orders to embark on a fool's errand. It also carried assurances from Hitler that, upon his safe return to Germany, he would be reinstated as the Führer's immediate successor. Closing the letter, he placed it between the pages of the journal. He made no attempt to hide the forlorn expression on his face as the Mercedes turned into the busy airfield. *God protect me as I do what must be done.*

The car made its way between agitated soldiers who were loading cargo onto various planes and trucks. No matter how busy they were, protocol dictated they stand to attention and salute when Hess's car passed. It stopped alongside a Messerschmitt 110 fighter plane parked just off the runway. Pintsch got out of the passenger seat and tried to open the back door.

'Give me a moment, will you?'

'Of course, Herr Reich Minister.' Pintsch walked away from the car to give his boss some privacy.

Hess closed the journal, snapped its fastener, and locked it. He placed the key on the seat beside him and reached down to place the journal by his feet. 'Remind me of the sequence, Sommer,' Hess asked the driver.

Without looking at his boss, Sommer recited the combination of the secret compartment under the floor. 'Raise the armrest on the left-hand side and lift up the seat slightly.'

Hess did as he was instructed and waited for the click.

The previous day, when he had taken possession of the car at the Reich's Chancellery in Berlin, Sommer had taken the precaution of having the secret compartment fitted by a discreet furniture maker of his acquaintance. He had taken the same precaution for all the vehicles his boss had used during his time as Deputy Führer. The furniture maker had spent all night on the job and ended up with a mechanical hideaway that was undetectable to anyone who didn't know it was there.

Hess pulled away the carpet and groped around the floorboards for the latch. He opened the secret compartment and placed the journal inside. Closing the compartment, he replaced the carpet and straightened his uniform as he looked ahead. He grabbed the key and handed it to Sommer, who was still sitting in the driver's seat. The two men looked at each other for a moment, as if to acknowledge a secret pact to which they alone were privy. Hess patted the young officer on the shoulder and smiled. 'Guard this with your life, Sommer. If I am not back in three days, you know what to do.'

Sommer placed the key in his uniform pocket. Hess got out of the car and smiled at his adjutant. He took another letter out of his tunic pocket and handed it to Pintsch.

'See that this is delivered after I take off.'

Pintsch accepted the letter, which was addressed to Hitler, and stood to attention. He said, 'The world will remember your actions today, Herr Reich Minister. The lives of millions are in your hands.'

Hess made an about-turn and walked towards the plane, eyeing the craft up and down as he went. He returned the 'Heil Hitler' salute of a nearby flight mechanic and kneeled to inspect the wheels.

Hess had trained on the two-seater twin-engine aircraft for about seven months under the watchful eye of Wilhelm Stör, the chief test pilot at Messerschmitt, and his colleague, Helmut Kaden. He had logged many cross-country flights and felt confident he could complete the task at hand. With a smile on his face, he remembered Hitler's idea to publicly prohibit him from flying so he could later disavow all knowledge of Hess's actions. It took him a while, but he found a loyal ground crew that was willing to turn a blind eye to his activities and keep the mission a secret. He had chosen his favourite plane and had it modified to include a radio compass, oxygen delivery system and long-range fuel tanks.

Hess considered it ironic that his nemesis, Hermann Göring, was a proponent of the Messerschmitt Bf 110. It was developed in the 1930s and was intended for use by the Luftwaffe during the war. It would normally be armed with two MG FF 20 mm cannons, four 7.92 mm MG 17 machine guns and one 7.92 mm MG 15 machine gun, but Hess had these weapons removed to make the plane lighter. After all, this was supposed to be a mission of peace, not war. The Bf 110's lack of agility in the air was a weakness that Hess considered irrelevant considering the current mission.

Colonel Kurt Schmidt, the chief of the Met Office, sauntered out of his hut, followed by Kaden and Willy Messerschmitt himself.

'Greetings, Herr Hess,' said Messerschmitt. To the annoyance of high-ranking Nazis, the renowned aircraft engineer and designer always made a point of avoiding references to military or political rank.

Hess opted to disregard the slight and shook the designer's hand with a smile. He also shook hands with Kaden and thanked him for being so patient during his many hours of training. All three men looked up at the plane and admired her lean design.

They turned their attention to Schmidt when the colonel coughed and tapped his chest with his clipboard for dramatic effect. Hess did not like the expression on the colonel's face—he couldn't bear another cancellation and braced for the worst. The flight had been postponed several times already due to mechanical problems and inclement weather, but Hess was determined that today was the day. Tonight would be a full moon, and his astrology charts showed that the planets were uniquely aligned for an immediate departure.

Schmidt looked at his notes and said, 'Outbreaks of rain or drizzle are expected over the North Sea and will become persistent, and sometimes heavy, in coastal districts along the northeast of Great Britain...'.

That doesn't sound so bad, Hess thought, as he allowed a frown to cross his face.

'Patches of fog will affect the coast of Scotland. Otherwise mainly dry, with early patches of mist and drizzle largely dying out, allowing some bright, or short sunny intervals, to develop locally. Lowest temperatures seven to ten degrees Celsius, with moderate to fresh southerly breezes.'

Hess waited for the colonel to continue, but then he could wait no longer. 'So, am I cleared for take-off?'

'Yes, Herr Reich Minister, you are cleared for take-off.'

Hess raised his arm and punched the air with his fist. He

allowed himself a triumphant smile and gestured to
Sommer to join him. He took off his tunic and handed it to
his driver. Kaden and Messerschmitt clapped their hands in
unison, but it was unclear if they were happy for Hess or if
they were just glad their part in his secret mission was at an
end.

'The time has come, gentlemen.' Hess placed his hands
on the rails at the side of the aircraft and climbed the steps
to the cockpit.

The assembled onlookers watched in horror as Hess
slipped on the first footrest and banged his knee on the
aircraft. They waited as the senior Nazi grabbed hold of the
rails again and made a second attempt to reach the cockpit.
Everyone breathed a sigh of relief when Hess finally made
it to his seat in the cockpit and began the pre-flight check.

'You carry with you the hopes of the Reich, Herr Reich
Minister,' Sommer said, handing Hess a bag of supplies.

With a final check of the instrument panel, Hess
switched on the ignition and tested the wing flaps. After
the mechanics removed the wheel blocks, he eased the
aircraft away from the building. Guiding the plane across
the air base, he settled at the near end of the runway. At
fourteen minutes to six on the evening of May 10, Hess
applied full throttle and began his take-off run. Over a
dozen people watched as the fighter plane ascended and
disappeared into the sun.

Day One

1

Castel Gandolfo, Summer Residence of the Pope, Present Day

DISTRACTED by the bright colours in the garden, Monsignor Marcus Nee looked out of the library window and admired the flora radiating in the midday sun. The glimmering vista was in sharp contrast to the gloomy darkness of the library, with its musty odour and towering shelves of ancient books.

'Where's the hospital?' Luigi Manetti asked, making sure to pronounce every word clearly.

'Why do you want to go to the hospital?' Marcus asked.

'Because I'm sick.'

'Very good, Now, move on to the next chapter.'

Marcus didn't consider himself a teacher, but he made an exception in Luigi's case. The boy had fallen in with a criminal element and been kicked out of every school he had ever attended. But he loved his mother, so Marcus decided that was a good enough reason to give the boy another chance.

He had considered conducting the lesson on the terrace, where they could enjoy the sun and the fresh air, but the boy needed the discipline and quiet reflection that only the library could offer. At Marcus's behest, Luigi had agreed to give up his life of crime to work in the Barberini Gardens as a part-time gardener. He had agreed to visit the library twice a week for English lessons, though Marcus suspected it had more to do with Maria, his 21-year-old housekeeper, than his desire to better himself.

It seemed more than a coincidence that the only two days Luigi was free for lessons corresponded with Maria's work schedule, and Marcus had caught the pair of them flirting more than once. He was willing to turn a blind eye if it kept Luigi out of the clutches of the local Mafiosi, who were, so far, happy to conduct their nefarious activities outside the boundaries of Castel Gandolfo.

About thirty kilometres south of Rome, Castel Gandolfo was considered just as much a part of Vatican City as Saint Peter's Square. It comprised three villas, a church and other buildings, all surrounded by thirty hectares of gardens. Marcus's apartment was in Barberini Palace, next door to the Pope's residence in the Apostolic Palace.

Marcus was just about to go on to the next chapter when Maria arrived to clear up the breakfast dishes. Luigi couldn't keep his eyes off the pretty girl, which prompted Marcus to tap his pencil on the boy's hand to get him to return his attention to the books.

'You can go now Maria, like a good girl,' Marcus said, turning his attention to Luigi. 'What does this say?'

'I like to be by the seaside.'

'Very good. Now read this passage to yourself.'

Marcus walked around his desk and sat on his leather chair. He glanced at his calendar and his eyes immediately focused on a date, circled in red, less than a week away. It was a date he had been dreading but one he could not ignore.

The silence was shattered by a loud knock on the door. Before Marcus could react, two priests entered and walked to the middle of the room. The older of the two, Father Salvatore, bowed his head and coughed. 'Forgive me, Monsignor.'

Marcus looked up and smiled. 'What is it, lads?'

'His Holiness has an urgent appointment, but we can't seem to extricate him from his current engagement. The prime minister of Canada has been waiting some time.'

'That's good to know,' Marcus said, winking at Luigi. 'What's it got to do with me?'

'We were hoping you could help us,' Father Salvatore stammered. 'You see, Signore Eamon's daily "confessional" with the Holy Father has run on longer than usual.' That Father Salvatore managed to inject extra sarcasm into the word 'confessional' was not lost on Marcus.

He never regretted bringing Eamon, his father, to live with him in Italy but he had to admit the old man was sometimes more trouble than he was worth. It made sense to relocate him to a warmer climate, where he could keep an eye on him, and rent out their farm in the Aran Islands.

Eamon's main role was to manage the small Irish pub they had purchased in the local town. It was supposed to keep him occupied and get him out of the residence regularly. Marcus had to admit that although it kept the old man out of trouble, it was also like hiring a wolf to manage a flock of sheep.

When Eamon had become bored of managing the pub, he had delegated more and more responsibility to his assistant manager. Nobody noticed when he had drifted into another role that turned out to be just as important. It transpired that Eamon and the Pope were kindred spirits, two lonely men of the same age who enjoyed each other's company. The Pope needed friendship as much as anyone and the Vatican staff had seen the benefit of having someone on the premises with whom the Holy Father could socialise.

'I see,' said Marcus. 'And you want me to go over there and separate my father and the Holy Father?'

Father Salvatore shuffled his feet and looked toward the floor. His colleague, Father Allman, stepped forward. 'In a manner of speaking, yes.'

'Very well.' Marcus rose from his desk and looked at Luigi. 'You did very well today, lad. Go back to the gardens and resume your duties. I will expect you at the same time on Tuesday.'

Marcus turned and approached Salvatore and Allman. He was taller than the two priests and at least ten years younger, and he possessed an air of authority they lacked. His dark hair, which was a little longer than most priests would tolerate, was greying at the temples. His piercing green eyes emitted warmth and compassion to most people caught in their gaze, but not to Salvatore and Allman.

'You go on ahead and I'll meet you there. I have to change into my cassock.'

Opening the double doors that led to the terrace, Marcus walked out into the sunshine. He didn't care for the condescending tone Salvatore and Allman adopted whenever they had to speak to him about his father. But he understood their position and couldn't blame them for being annoyed. They were senior officials who had worked for the Vatican for decades, serving several popes.

He was also aware that his 'colleagues' at the Vatican were jealous of his swift elevation to his position as Director of the Pontifical Villas of Castel Gandolfo. It sometimes embarrassed him that he held a more senior position than other, more experienced, clergymen. But he couldn't help it if Pope John Paul III trusted him more than he trusted his other advisors. There was nothing else for it but to work harder to get along with them.

After changing into his cassock, Marcus walked out the tall doors of his apartment and into an austere corridor linking Barberini Palace with the Papal Palace. He disliked wearing the cassock, but the Holy Father had ordered all his priests to observe the traditional niceties while serving on the grounds of the Vatican.

As he marched down the passageway, his leather shoes made an unmerciful racket on the stone floor. When he reached the end, the glass doors separating the two villas were opened by one of the two posted Swiss Guards. He crossed the Papal threshold and found himself in an ornate hallway.

The contrast between the two villas could not have been more apparent. The marble floor was covered in a lush, dark blue carpet, and the walls were adorned with the paintings of Titian, Tintoretto, Caravaggio, Poussin, Rubens, Vermeer and Rembrandt.

The taste of Marcus's predecessor had run very much to the Baroque period, but the Pope himself favoured the Venetian School. Marcus made a mental note to brighten up the place with some post-impressionists like Cézanne or van Gogh.

He looked out the large window onto the magnificent Barberini Gardens and considered the course of events that had led him to this splendid demesne.

Marcus had known Pope John Paul III for more than 20 years, when the senior priest was Archbishop Antonio Abbaticchio, the Papal Nuncio to Ireland. Father Antonio, as he liked to be called, took Marcus under his wing and became his mentor during his time at the seminary in Maynooth. Antonio had persuaded Marcus's tutors at Saint Patrick's College to let the young student continue his studies in Rome after only four years in Maynooth. Marcus had spent two years at the Irish College, by which time Father Antonio had become a major player in the hierarchy of the Church. The Italian was impressed with Marcus's grasp of theology and political science as well as his gift for languages, especially Latin and Italian. He had always thought Marcus could best serve the priesthood in a political capacity in the Vatican. It wasn't long before the young Irishman learned the finer points of papal politics.

Marcus had been an exceptional student, a fact first noticed by his teachers on the Aran Islands, his birthplace on the west coast of Ireland. They had seen that he'd been leagues ahead of the other students, and they had arranged for him to attend a secondary school run by the Jesuits in Galway city. Saint Ignatius College had not only encouraged Marcus to hone his rowing skills, it had also helped him to clarify his vocation and smooth his path into the priesthood. From there, he had studied theology and political science at Trinity College before attending the seminary in Maynooth, where he'd met Father Antonio.

When Antonio had been elevated to the rank of cardinal, one of his first duties had been to send Marcus back home to the Aran Islands to replace Father O'Flaherty, an old priest who was past retirement age. That suited Marcus fine because his father needed help around the farm after losing his leg in a farming accident.

Later, when he returned to the pomp and political intrigue of the Eternal City, Marcus was ready to take his place at his mentor's side and become his most trusted advisor. His gift for languages and ability to diplomatically obfuscate led to his appointment as the cardinal's personal secretary, and the occasional stint at the Vatican's diplomatic service as a liaison to visiting dignitaries.

Marcus fiddled with the golden crucifix hanging from his neck and recalled with glee the many tussles he'd had with dignitaries from the United States, France, China and other important nations who thought they could do and see whatever they liked inside the Vatican. He smiled about the time he'd frog-marched Donald Rumsfeld out of the Sistine Chapel while his Secret Service detail looked on in horror.

Recently, when the Holy Father had offered him his choice of positions, he'd chosen Castel Gandolfo because of its laid-back atmosphere and its famous gardens. He could think of no better pursuits at the end of the working day than to walk in the gardens or plot the stars in the observatory. He was also drawn to the papal outpost because it seemed like a good place to bring Eamon, who needed plenty of distractions to keep him out of trouble.

But the management of the Pope's summer residence was an important job that demanded his full-time attention. It was an onerous task and Marcus needed all his wits about him to do it properly.

Unfortunately, the Pope's relationship with Eamon often took him away from his official duties and Marcus feared the Vatican officials were losing their patience.

He crossed the hallway and climbed the marble staircase to the second floor, where the Pope's private apartments were situated. When he reached the top of the stairs, Marcus was confronted with a provocatively naked marble statue by the early Renaissance sculptor Donatello, a horrific sight that always sent shivers up his spine. Salvatore and Allman were waiting for Marcus as he walked past the two Swiss Guards standing at attention with their halberds raised. He waited for a moment in front of the door to gather himself.

Due to the abundance of priceless art and antique furniture on display, the Swiss Guards were always on duty at the Papal Palace, even when the Pope was not in residence. Marcus was glad of their presence, but he was grateful the spartan décor of his own living quarters required no such suffocating security.

He straightened his cassock and knocked on the tall doors. Without waiting for a reply, he swung the doors open and walked into the spacious apartment, followed by Salvatore and Allman.

'They are in the Holy Father's study,' said Father Salvatore, pointing at the door in the corner of the room.

Marcus smiled at the two priests and walked over to the door. He knocked, opened the door and entered. While he waited to be summoned, he surveyed the scene before him. The floor was covered in antique Persian rugs and several French Regency-style ebonized tables that held the Pope's collection of Carrara marble figures. One side of the room was taken up with a desk and an eighteenth-century Louis Bas grand piano.

Two men were sitting around a scaled model of an ancient, fortified city, complete with miniature soldiers, trees and castles. The model, made of wood and *papier-mâché*, was resting on a large table in the corner of the room.

Eamon and Pope John Paul III were playing with hundreds of painted sixty-millimetre metal soldiers that were dotted around the model.

'Come in, Marcus,' said the pontiff. 'You are just in time to see the forces of Henry II of Cyprus, King of Jerusalem, defeat the Mamluk invaders.'

Marcus approached the Pope, kneeled on one knee and kissed the Ring of the Fisherman on his outstretched hand. He stood up and admired the impressive model. The historical accuracy of the ancient city amazed him as well as the incredible attention to detail.

'The Siege of Acre in 1291, if I'm not mistaken.' Marcus reached out his arm to grab a Mamluk standard bearer, but Eamon slapped his hand before he could grab it.

'Get your hands off that,' Eamon shouted. 'The mighty Sultan Khalil needs all the troops he can muster if he is to destroy the Crusaders and the Knights Templar.'

'This was presented to me by Nelson Mandela, a great and honourable man,' said the Pope.

Marcus retracted his hand and glowered at his father. 'Well, the Mamluk army is going to have to do without your help for a while.' Marcus winked at his father and then turned his attention to the pontiff. 'Your Holiness, I'm afraid I have to drag my father away on urgent business.'

'Very well, my son.' The Pope returned the figure of Henry II to its proper position on the model. 'I know I am late for some important meeting or other. Who is it today?'

'I believe it's the prime minister of Canada, Holy Father.'

The Pope sighed and eased himself off his chair. 'How are you getting on with your new appointment?' he asked.

'It is a challenge, Holy Father.' Marcus bowed his head. 'But one I am very much enjoying.'

'I believe you are the first Irishman to hold the position of Director of the Pontifical Villas of Castel Gandolfo.'

'Yes, Holy Father.'

'Now, if only you could use your powers to sneak in some of that famous Irish whiskey, we'd all be a little happier.'

'I'll see what can be done, Holy Father.'

The Pope picked up a figure of a Mamluk soldier with outstretched sword and turned his attention to Eamon. 'You don't get out of it that easily, Sultan Nee,' he said, throwing the figure in Eamon's direction. 'I hope this will give you the inspiration to improve your strategy before your encounter with the Crusaders tomorrow.'

'I have a few more tricks up my sleeve, Holy Father,' Eamon said as he caught the figure.

Marcus kneeled to kiss the Pope's ring once again before he and his father departed. As they left, Father Salvatore came rushing in with the Pope's white vestments.

When they were back in the corridor next to the ghastly Donatello statue, Marcus placed his hands gently on his father's shoulders and gave him a little shake. 'How many times have I told you to stop taking up all of his time?'

'It's not my fault, Marcus,' Eamon pleaded. 'He practically begged me to play with him. You can't blame the man for wanting to have some fun every now and then. It's like a bloody morgue around here sometimes.'

Eamon struggled to keep his balance under the strain of his son's interrogation. He shifted his weight between his real leg and his artificial limb.

Once tall and elegant, Eamon had become withered and scrawny in old age. But he lost none of his poise, and his cold blue eyes seemed to mellow when he smiled. Except for the dentures at the front of his mouth, all his teeth were his own. He always wore a tweed cap and matching jacket with leather patches stitched into the elbows.

Marcus let go of his father and guided him down the staircase. 'All I'm saying is, be aware of his schedule and make sure he makes his appointments on time. We kept the Dalai Lama waiting an hour and a half last week because of your shenanigans.'

Eamon stopped half-way down the staircase and looked at his son. 'Have you made up your mind about Sperlonga?' he asked, referring to the upcoming nuptials of their friends Willie and Sarah in the seaside resort.

'This is neither the time nor the place.'

Marcus didn't need to be reminded of the wedding. He recalled with devastating clarity how his heart sank when Willie asked him to officiate over the ceremony. His delight at being asked to officiate over their marriage ceremony was matched only by the pang of regret that festered somewhere deep inside him about the road not travelled. He'd had his chance to have a life with Sarah years before and he chose an ecclesiastical path instead. While he never regretted becoming a priest, he always wondered about what might have been. He still couldn't believe they would be married in less than a week. It seemed like only yesterday that he and Sarah shared a grotty bedsit in Dublin and struggled to make the rent. And now he was the director of the Pope's summer residence and she was marrying his best friend at the hotel they owned in Sperlonga.

Day Two

2

Rome, Italy

THE cool conditioned air inside the Nuova Fiera di Roma exhibition centre was a welcome relief for the hundreds of visitors who had come in from the sweltering Roman heat. The glass doors opened and closed automatically as motor enthusiasts entered and exited the massive auditorium. Fuori Serie, the annual vintage car and motorcycle trade fair, had been in full swing all week but the weekend crowd had filled the centre to near capacity. The show, which was taking place throughout several pavilions, featured vintage, classic, and sports cars, spare parts and accessories, motorbikes, model-making gear, material for restoration as well as booths promoting rallies and other events. On a local radio show, one of the organisers had boasted that every "petrol head" in Italy would be in attendance.

The test-driving section seemed to be a big hit. Despite the heat of the outdoor track, people were waiting in a long line to test-drive the new Jeep Wrangler. Drivers took on the obstacle course and thirty-five-degree hill, and most of them seemed not to mind that the music was being pumped out at an ear-splitting volume.

A whole section was dedicated to luxury and super cars. They all looked much the same, but the crowds seemed more interested in the scantily clad models draped over the motors. The centre was full of beautiful waifs who were either swooning next to the latest super cars or shimmying about, being ogled by randy teenagers. All the big car manufacturers used the show to unveil their new-age concept cars, many of which would never make it into production. Still, it gave the audience a glimpse into the future.

Some of the manufacturers even gave away free merchandise: Fiat was giving Mini iPods as gifts; Ferrari reps were passing out polo shirts; and the glamorous models at other booths were handing out free bags. Mitsubishi gave visitors the chance to win hats and other prizes if they could fold paper airplanes and fly them into a chute. Subaru allowed visitors to play with toy cars in a little town model. Volkswagen had a stunning interactive exhibit and they were giving out special plastic cars.

The motorcycle section was full of customised motorcycles, Quad bikes, ATVs, scooters and even a few Harley-Davidsons. Raffles and non-car related items were also available— visitors could get their shoes polished and jewellery cleaned as they browsed the exhibits. Many of the more expensive cars were either locked, roped off, or under one-on-one supervision by intimidating blonde women, so the visitors were kept at arm's length. Most of the other exhibits were either displayed behind glass or on rotating stages.

The north wing was dedicated to electric and hybrid cars, classic vintage automobiles, old police cars and some historic automobiles. In this section, the largest crowd of all was gathered around an exhibit featuring a black vintage Mercedes-Benz limousine. The ancient beast was standing on a revolving stage, next to a large window that overlooked a busy street. The chrome bodywork gleamed in the spotlight as the crowd looked on in awe.

Luigi Manetti was standing next to the car, waxing lyrical about its illustrious history. But Luigi Manetti wasn't the name on his name tag¬—it was Enzo Abbiatti. He was wearing a purple blazer, a white shirt and a purple tie—the same uniform as every employee at the show. His mother would have said he looked very handsome, even if purple was not among her favourite colours.

Luigi had spent several days learning about the car. He stole a brochure from the exhibition hall a few days earlier and did hours of research on the Internet.

'This classic beauty was the official car of Rudolf Hess, the infamous Nazi who stayed in Berlin's Spandau Prison until his death in 1987,' the young man said with an air of authority. 'The Mercedes-Benz 770 limousine you see before you is the actual car he used from the outbreak of World War II, until he embarked on his mysterious flight to Scotland in 1941. Sometimes referred to as *Grosser*, because of its size, the car was fitted with mine-proof floor armour, as well as thick bulletproof glass and bodywork.'

Luigi reached in through the open door and switched on the ignition. The in-line eight-cylinder engine roared into life, and the crowd applauded as he stuck his foot in and revved up the engine.

'As you can see, the car runs just as well as it did all those years ago,' he gushed with pride. In one orchestrated move, Luigi climbed through the open door, put his foot on the clutch, and pushed the gear lever into first.

Luigi was sure Monsignor Marcus would have been proud of his ability to remember all those details on the old car, but that couldn't stop the pang of regret he felt for betraying his tutor and breaking his promise to stop stealing.

He waited for the revolving stage to bring the car into optimum alignment with the window, then he let out the clutch and hit the accelerator hard. He closed his eyes and kept hold of the steering wheel as the car roared forward, shattering the window. Glass flew everywhere and passers-by scurried as the car landed in the middle of the street and screeched to a halt, causing the oncoming traffic to swerve and crash. He revved up the engine again and stomped on the accelerator. Glancing at his rear-view mirror, he watched as some of the exhibition-goers walked out onto the street through the broken window to survey the damage.

As the car travelled north along Via Portuense, a passing police car stopped and turned to pursue. The police switched on the sirens and lights, picking up speed as it followed Luigi. The black Mercedes was faster than it looked and easily outpaced the police car. Two more police cars appeared out of cross streets and joined the pursuit. Luigi shifted gears and smiled at the ease with which the old car outran its pursuers. He swerved to avoid an oncoming car and just missed a pedestrian crossing the street. Several more police cars joined the chase, but they couldn't get any closer to the Mercedes.

Every time the car broke a red light, it caused minor crashes and consternation. The chasing police cars barely made it through the clogged intersections as they continued their pursuit. Luigi struggled to control the car and turn the cumbersome steering wheel.

The giant limousine was not designed to turn corners and manoeuvre tight spaces at high speeds. Luigi realized he had to get on a straight road where he could build up speed. He could see the Fiumicino Airport Motorway up ahead, and he knew if he could reach it, he'd be home and dry. Turning the car into a sharp bend, he just missed several oncoming cars as he entered an old cobblestoned avenue.

He cursed aloud when he saw the green, open-top double-decker bus coming towards him from the other end of the avenue. The driver of the bus, a thin man who looked many years beyond retirement age, was first to react. The old man turned his steering wheel to avoid the oncoming limousine, causing the bus to tilt on its side. It remained balanced on two wheels for what seemed like an age, before it continued its tilting motion and rested on the buildings on the driver's side of the avenue. The tourists on the upper deck of the bus didn't seem fazed—they appeared jubilant as they climbed off the bus onto the roof of the building on which the bus was leaning.

With just enough room to spare, Luigi slipped the Mercedes past the bus, avoiding an electricity pole.

The first police cars to reach the scene crashed into the bus, and the police officers in the second cars managed to escape their vehicles just before the following cars crashed into them. The officers watched as the Mercedes zoomed away.

Luigi was relieved to find the airport motorway on-ramp, and he eased his way into the traffic heading east. The motorway was not congested because he was travelling away from the airport and towards the city. He had practiced the route several times in his old Fiat Uno, so he knew the way off by heart.

With its gleaming chrome bumpers and enormous headlights, the big black limousine stood out from all the modern cars on the motorway. Luigi cared little about history, but he was aware that old things were often worth a lot of money. Knowing full well he was untouchable on the motorway, he began to relax and enjoy the ride. He shifted into fifth gear supercharge and laughed as the Mercedes passed everything in sight. The other cars were just a blur as he zipped along.

Luigi had been stealing cars since he was old enough to spit. It started out as a bit of fun, and then he realised it allowed him to bring money home to his mother. Lately, though, he had been trying to mend his ways and get an honest job. It was the only way to live up to the potential Monsignor Marcus saw in him and also win the affections of Maria. His love life would not sit well with his life of crime, he thought. But Silvio Montagna, the local *capo* of the Gallico di Palmi crime family, cared little for his love life. The Mountain, as he was known to his enemies, was reluctant to lose Luigi's services. He had made it clear that Luigi's mother was more likely to live a long and healthy life if the young man did him a service from time to time.

This is the last job, he told himself as he guided the monster Mercedes along the motorway, *no matter what The Mountain says*. When the signs for the A90 exit came into view, Luigi got ready to turn right onto the GRA, the ring road that encircled Rome. He looked at his watch and congratulated himself on the cunning simplicity of his plan. Shifting down a gear, he followed the motorway to the right. Rome was spread out on the left and, even to his cynical eyes, its ancient buildings looked enchanting and majestic in the distance. Maria was never far from his thoughts as he considered what the future had in store for them. His mother would approve if they got married and had children, but even Luigi knew that wasn't likely unless he got an honest job.

After ten more kilometres, he exited the GRA and took a right onto the Via Appia Nuova. As he headed south, parallel to the Appian Way—the world's first road—it occurred to him that Maria might like to see his latest 'toy'. Perhaps she would even like to join him for an afternoon drive along the lake. The Mountain could wait a little longer for his car. test-driving

3

THE Nuova Fiera di Roma exhibition hall was full of *Carabinieri*, forensic analysts and TV crews when Detective Sergeant Scot Mancuso and Detective Giovanni Rossi finished questioning the witnesses. Yellow police tape criss-crossed the broken window to form a large 'X' on the side of the building. More Carabinieri was outside directing traffic.

When he left the Detroit Police Department, Mancuso never imagined he would end up in a place like this. He had signed up for the Interpol Italian Central Bureau hoping to rub shoulders with celebrity criminals, wayward rock stars and eccentric diplomats, not sifting through oil-stained evidence.

Mancuso took a sip of coffee from a paper cup as he surveyed the scene. Spitting the coffee back into the cup, his face contorted in reaction to the foul taste. It was ironic that even though his love of Italian coffee had been one of the reasons he had decided to move to Italy, he had been unable to find a decent cup of coffee since he got here. He turned his back on the TV cameras as their operators jostled for position and hoped he wouldn't have to speak to them—not yet anyway.

Catching a glimpse at his own reflection in one of the large windows, he noted that his light brown hair looked greyer than usual under the camera lights. Tall and stout, he had recently acquired a protruding belly from consuming too much tiramisu and sweetened cappuccino. The difference in style between Mancuso and his Italian counterparts could not have been more striking. In comparison, the American looked like a homeless person who had just woken up from a night sleeping on a park bench. Suits were not his thing, but he got away with a shirt and jeans, as long as he wore a smart jacket. Since immigrating to Italy, he had taken to wearing a Texas-style buckle on his belt to make himself look more American.

It had been ten years since he left Detroit to live in the land of his ancestors. Raised in a proud Italian family in the Highland Park neighbourhood of Motown, he learned how to speak Italian fluently so he could communicate with his grandmother. As Interpol had needed experienced detectives, he'd applied for the job in Rome and never looked back.

He did nothing to hide the anxious expression on his face as his partner approached.

Unlike Mancuso, Rossi was decked out from head to toe in designer apparel and his jet-black hair was perfectly groomed. He and Mancuso had worked together at Interpol for more than six years, on cases that had a foreign angle. Thanks to his time in the United States, Rossi spoke good English and saved everyone the trouble of deciphering Mancuso's southern Italian. They made a great team—Rossi dealt with the Italian police and witnesses, while Mancuso worked the evidence.

'We got nothing on the security cameras, Scotty,' Rossi said. 'The suspect knew where they all were and made sure to hide his face. One of the security guards got a good look at him. He was Italian. About five-ten and in his early twenties. We managed to get a clean set of prints on the podium, so we might be lucky.'

'He worked here, right?' Mancuso asked. 'Surely someone knows him.'

'The man who was supposed to be working at the Mercedes exhibit is called Enzo Abbiatti. He was attacked at his home last night and spent most of today gagged and tied to his bed. I sent a unit of the *Carabinieri* to his home to interview him. He said a man wearing a hood broke into his apartment while he was having dinner and tied him up. The man finished his dinner and polished off a fifty-euro bottle of Chianti before he left. He also took his uniform, complete with name tag.'

'You think this guy is professional?'

'Either that or he's been doing it so long he got good at it.'

'And the car?'

'The car belonged to General John P. McNamara, United States Army retired.' Rossi consulted his notes. 'He left it to the museum in his will. He liberated it from Germany after the war and brought it to Italy when he was stationed here in the fifties. It managed to outrun half the cop cars in the city.'

'It had to be stolen to order, right?'

Rossi nodded in agreement. 'The *Carabinieri* stayed with him until he got on the motorway. He caused a bus to crash, and then they lost him. They don't even know which way he went.'

'Send the *Carabinieri* to turn over all the known chop shops. Someone is bound to know who stole it. I'll talk to my Mafiosi snitches and see what they come up with.'

'This one's going to be a real stinker,' said Rossi. 'I hear the British Embassy's involved.'

Mancuso frowned and watched as his partner walked away. He strolled around the podium again and tried to re-enact the crime in his head. *He's got balls, I'll give him that*, Mancuso thought. He was lost in his own world when a tap on the shoulder brought him back to reality. Turning around, he realised he had wandered too close to the police cordon, and too close to the gaggle of reporters. He cursed to himself when he saw a familiar face in front of him.

'Detective, I'm Joanne Cory from CNN,' said the reporter, who thrust her microphone right up to his face. 'Do you have any leads in the carjacking?'

'It's detective *sergeant*, Joanne. And no, we don't have any leads.' Mancuso had had several run-ins with this reporter before and he was in no mood to volunteer any information that might further her career.

'Is it true the mafia might be behind this?' the reporter pressed. 'Specifically, Silvio Montagna from the Gallico di Palmi crime family, who is known to have a lucrative sideline in stolen vintage cars.'

'We'll fill you in when we have more information, Joanne,' Mancuso said. 'In the meantime, it doesn't do us any good to speculate.'

Mancuso was already backing away when the reporter asked her next question. 'Do you know where the car in now, detective? It can't be that easy to hide.'

Mancuso smirked at the reporter as he backed away. He looked up and was surprised to see his partner again so soon. 'That was quick.'

'Are we finished here?' Rossi asked.

'Why'—Mancuso was irritated by the question—'am I in the way?'

'There's been a murder on the outskirts of the city that needs our urgent attention. The local police dropped it on our laps when they realised the body might be British.'

'Jesus Christ, I can't be in two places at the same time.' He took one last look at the crime scene and followed his partner out of the auditorium.

The police siren was on full blast as Rossi drove the Fiat Tipo along the motorway. Mancuso feared for his safety as Rossi squeezed the Tipo between two larger cars and accelerated past them.

'You like using the police siren so you can drive even more recklessly than normal,' said Mancuso.

'What's the point of being a cop if we can't go crazy sometimes.'

'There's normal crazy and then there's Italian crazy.'

'Stop being such a pussy and enjoy the ride,' Rossi said as they were overtaken by a Ferrari. He shifted into fourth gear and gave chase.

As they crossed the River Tiber and turned right onto the Circonvallazione Meridonale, the Ferrari grew smaller as it accelerated farther away. Mancuso was glad the Polizia di Stato was too cash-strapped to instal traffic cameras on the motorways. It was not the first time he had noticed that Italian institutional corruption had worked in his favour.

'You remember my friend Rossetti, who works for Polizia di Stato?' said Rossi.

Mancuso nodded his head.

'Those cocksuckers get to drive around in Lamborghini Gallardos.'

Mancuso nodded again and hoped he never had to ride shotgun with Rossi in a Lamborghini Gallardo.

As they approached the turnoff for SR6, Rossi gave up the chase and shifted down to third gear. He exited the motorway and turned right toward Tor Bella Monaca.

Tor Bella Monaca was a drug-infested, crime-ridden part of Rome that was seldom mentioned on the tourist maps. When he got out of the car and surveyed the scene, Mancuso was not happy about rooting around a decomposing body in a desolate wasteland.

This decomposing body belonged to a British national, which is why Interpol had been called in. The *Carabinieri* was more than happy to hand over the case, as long as one of its officers was part of the investigation.

'So, why are we here, Dino?' Mancuso asked the forensic pathologist.

'She was murdered. Blunt force trauma. She sustained two or three blows to the back of the head. Her face also shows signs of a beating.'

'What about the murder weapon?'

'Something hard and heavy,' said Dino. 'Maybe a tire iron or a crowbar. She's been dead for no more than an hour and a half. There's no identification and the fingerprint search turned up nothing.'

'Why do we think she's British?'

'Her blouse and skirt were purchased at Debenhams, a chain of stores found in Great Britain and Ireland,' said Rossi.

'She could be Irish?' Mancuso suggested.

'Unlikely. The price is written on the skirt label. It's in pound sterling ... the Irish use the euro currency, same as us.'

'Something is missing.' Mancuso looked at the body. 'She looks like a businesswoman but there's no sign of a phone, a handbag or even car keys.'

'It's unlikely she was killed here,' said Dino. 'If there was a struggle in this dump, her clothes would be dirtier and probably torn.'

'It would be difficult for someone to sneak up on her here,' said Mancuso. 'But what was she doing here in the first place?'

'That's your problem,' said Dino. 'I'll be able to tell you more about the murder weapon when I get her back to the lab.'

The two Interpol detectives turned to look for the cause of a commotion behind them.

The Primo Capitano of the *Carabinieri* walked through the police cordon, flashing his badge. He was followed by an attractive blonde woman wearing a smart business suit, almost identical to that worn by the victim.

'Mancuso, this is Jessica Barkman,' the police chief said. 'She is a special liaison from the British Embassy. She will be helping us with our investigation of the stolen car.'

The woman manoeuvred through the assembled police officers and stretched out her arm to shake hands with Mancuso. He ignored her and grabbed the police chief by the arm, dragging him to the side. 'What's going on here, sir? Since when do we work with foreign governments?'

'Don't give me a hard time on this, Mancuso. The Ministry of Foreign Affairs is crawling all over me about the stolen Mercedes. Apparently, even the prime minister is involved. The British government wants us to find that fucking car.'

Mancuso looked over at Jessica, who was smiling at him. 'What do the Brits care about a stolen vintage car?'

'How should I know?' said the police chief. 'Just do as I say. Besides, she might be able to help with your murdered British national.' The police chief left as Rossi handed Mancuso a sheet of paper.

'The results came back from the print we got on the podium,' said Rossi. 'It belongs to Luigi Manetti, a low-ranking scumbag in the Gallico di Palmi crime family. He's a known car thief with a rap sheet as long as my *pene*. Pardon my French, Miss Barkman.'

'It sounded Italian to me.' Jessica stretched out her arm again and smiled as she waited for Mancuso to shake her hand.

'It looks like you'll have to fight it out with the mafia to get that car back.'

'I thought that was your job, detective,' said Jessica.

'You're kidding, right?' Mancuso said. 'That car's been disassembled and is on its way to Japan by now.'

Mancuso studied the woman for a moment and decided she was pretty, in an understated kind of way. She wasn't his type, of course, but then he didn't have a type.

'How can you be so sure, detective?' she asked.

'It's detective *sergeant*.'

'Sorry, detective sergeant, how can you be so sure the car was chopped up and sent to Japan?'

'This was a professional job. Professionals don't steal cars like this unless they already have a buyer. And the only people dumb enough and rich enough to want cars like this are the Japanese.'

'So, what are we going to do about it?'

'We aren't going to do anything about it. However, my team and I will track down the car and get back to you.'

'The car is very important to the British government. My masters would appreciate it if you would allow me to join your investigation team.'

'We are a very tight-knit team,' Mancuso said as he walked away. 'You would just be in the way. Give my partner your contact details.'

Day Three

4

Berlin, Germany

KARL Sommer hated when the television was switched on first thing in the morning. The last thing he wanted to hear when he got up for his breakfast was some talk-show host or news anchor shouting at him from the corner of the room. As he walked across the dining room, he realised the radio was also blasting away in the kitchen, resulting in a racket that was giving him a headache.

He had spoken to Ingrid about it a dozen times. This was the downside to living a double life designed to help him blend into normal society. But sharing his life with a loving wife was taking its toll. Sommer was not cut out for married life, even though he and Ingrid had lived together as husband and wife for more than twenty years. They lived together in the same house in the western suburbs of Berlin and they acted for all the world like a normal couple. They had slept together several dozen times, which was not enough for her to fulfil her duty and bear him a scion. It wasn't that Sommer didn't enjoy the comfort of women— it was just that he preferred them younger and less cooperative. Ingrid wasn't perfect, but she fulfilled the requirements of her initial brief: she made every attempt to conceive a child, and she performed the duties of a wife without complaint. Of course, she was well paid for her services and, it appeared to Sommer, she had nothing better to do.

In truth, Sommer was lucky to have her. After all, it wasn't easy to find a competent woman of pure German blood who would tolerate his proclivities. The framed photographs of Hitler and Hess were bad enough, but the giant swastika flag of the Third Reich was a bridge too far for most modern women. On balance, the advantages of having Ingrid around the house outweighed the disadvantages—he was far too busy to go through the considerable inconvenience of having to wash his own clothes, cook his food and clean the house. Then there were the social occasions, when having a charming wife by his side was a definite advantage.

On the bright side, Ingrid had a special talent for polishing medals. Sommer had once remarked at a dinner party that, if it were an Olympic event, Ingrid could polish medals for Germany. She made sure all the medals, buttons and insignia on his father's SS uniform, which he had kept draped on a tailor's dummy in the corner of the living room, were spick and span. He was sorry that neither the uniform nor the medals would ever again be seen in public.

But none of that mattered today. He had received wonderful news—news that he had been waiting to hear for more than a quarter of a century.

'Good morning,' Ingrid shouted from the kitchen as her husband sat on his favourite chair at the head of the dining table. Sommer poured himself a cup of coffee and sipped at it as he waited for his eggs and bacon to appear.

Even though Sommer always ate alone, the table was laid out with fine linen tablecloths and napkins, a silver tea set and an elegant set of china. The silver cutlery and the tableware bore the swastika and had been used at the Berghof by Hitler. Sommer purchased them from an arrogant American who claimed to have liberated them from the Führer's home in the Bavarian Alps. *It is a joyous morning*, Sommer thought, *perfect for a trip to Rome.*

Picking up his copy of *Die Zeit*, which was folded at the side of the table, he read the front page. The newspaper's centre-left editorials were tiresome, he always thought, but he appreciated its coverage of world events. Scanning the first few pages for news about Hess's car, he was annoyed to find it buried on page three. He read the report even though he had already been apprised of the salient details.

Sommer had been woken up by the phone call at just after two the previous afternoon. It had been an hour before he usually woke from his nap, so he had been groggy and irritated. But his eyes had lit up like a Christmas tree when the voice on the other end had informed him that the Deputy Führer's limousine had been found. Feeling wide awake, he had jumped out of bed to begin the necessary preparations. Most of the day and the following night had been spent making phone calls to key people in his organisation to make sure everyone knew what was expected of them. Grabbing a large suitcase from the top of his wardrobe, he had begun filling it with clothes and toiletries. Despite his wealth and gruelling work schedule, he always preferred to pack his own luggage and leave as little to chance as possible.

Dropping the newspaper back on the dining table, he ran through the plan again in his mind to ensure he had not overlooked any elements. When Ingrid arrived with the food, she gave her master a warm smile that wasn't reciprocated. She placed the food on the table in front of her employer. 'Please be careful, the plate is hot,' she said.

Sommer grunted and waited for Ingrid to leave so he could start his breakfast. As he picked up his knife and fork, he caught a glimpse of the picture of his father, Erich, on the mantelpiece. It had been taken in 1955 after his release by the Russians and had been the first photograph taken of him with the eye patch.

His father's account of how he had been relieved of his left eye years before by a group of over-zealous Russian soldiers still sent a shiver down Sommer's spine. As a keen archer and pheasant hunter, Erich had found it to be a terrible burden, but the worst part of it was seeing the reaction of others to his empty socket. Of course, he had been less concerned about their feelings than he was about how the missing eye affected him.

Sommer dipped a teaspoon into the jar of mayonnaise and spread it over his scrambled eggs. He was just about to load a mouthful of eggs into his mouth when something on the TV caught his eye. On CNN, a reporter was standing in front of a large broken window, behind which stood a cardboard sign with a picture of a vintage Mercedes-Benz limousine. Sommer picked up the remote control and turned up the volume. He was eager to see if there had been any developments in the story beyond what had already been reported to him by one of his agents in Italy and the account he had seen on German television.

'I'm standing here in the Nuova Fiera di Roma auditorium, where the annual Fuori Serie vintage car show is held. A remarkable car robbery took place here yesterday. A vintage automobile reputed to have belonged to Rudolf Hess, Hitler's deputy in the Nazi Party, was stolen in broad daylight.'

The phone on the dining room table rang and Sommer picked it up. He listened as the TV reporter continued his report.

The thief, who sped away with the vintage motor car before the police arrived on the scene, is believed to have acted alone.'

Sommer sipped his coffee and adjusted the volume on the television. 'Yes, I will be in the air in less than an hour. Is everything in place at your end?' He took another mouthful of coffee as he waited for the reply. 'Good, good. Make all the arrangements. I do not need to tell you how important it is that we retrieve the Reich Minister's documents.' He hung up the phone and looked at Ingrid, who was wiping away some imaginary dust on the Chinoiserie fireplace. As he stood, he glanced at the Louis-Philippe ormolu mantel clock and wondered if he would ever see it again.

'Did you enjoy your breakfast?' Ingrid asked as Sommer walked across the dining room. He walked out of the room and looked as if his mind was a million miles away. In all the years Sommer had been searching for the Deputy Führer's limousine, it had never occurred to him it might be in Italy. He had dedicated his life to fulfilling his father's oath to the Deputy Führer and finding the one document that would exonerate Hess and restore him to his rightful place in history.

Sommer remembered in vivid detail his father explaining how he had been arrested by the Gestapo after Hitler learned of Hess's flight to Scotland. Erich had been sent to a Gestapo detention facility in Berlin, where he had been beaten to within an inch of his life. He had refused to reveal the location of Hitler's letter to Hess, and his tormentors had been forced to conclude that he was either too stupid to have been taken into Hess's confidence or too clever to admit it.

At the start of Operation Barbarossa in the summer of 1941, Erich had been stripped of his SS rank, conscripted to the Wehrmacht and forced to join the long march into the Soviet Union. In January 1943, after months of watching his Sixth Army comrades die of starvation, disease, cold and suicide on the outskirts of Stalingrad, Erich had watched as the cowardly generals surrendered to the bloodthirsty Russians. At the time, he wondered how much different things would have been if Hess had been there to rally the troops with one of his rousing speeches and whip them up into a patriotic frenzy.

Erich had been identified as an SS officer by the blood-group tattoo on his arm and had been separated from his Wehrmacht comrades for 'special treatment'. His Russian tormentors incorrectly assumed he had valuable information, and they wasted little time removing his fingernails and gouging out his eye with a spoon. He watched in agony as they forced one of the other German POWs to eat his eye and wash it down with a mouthful of vodka. They kept him chained up in a damp room and subjected him to daily beatings. He was forced to eat cockroaches and rats for nourishment and, at night, listen to the tormented cries of his fellow prisoners.

After several months of torture and re-education, Erich had been sent to a Gulag in Northern Russia. He had barely survived his first winter in Siberia. With the help of his compatriots and his own desperate desire to once again see the Fatherland, he had managed to regain his strength. During the day, the German prisoners had been forced to build roads or lay railway tracks or whatever their Russian captors wanted. During the night, they had to sleep in the fields with no shelter from the elements or blankets to keep them warm. As the years passed, Erich had looked on helplessly every day as scores of prisoners succumbed to the harsh conditions and died. Every evening before they could light a fire and rest for the night, the surviving prisoners had to dig mass graves to bury the dead. Often times he had wished he would die in his sleep so that he would not have to wake up to another day in hell.

In the summer of 1955, more than twelve years after his surrender at the Battle of Stalingrad, Erich was released and allowed to return to Germany. Of the hundred and twenty thousand Germans who surrendered in Stalingrad, he had been one of only five thousand who made it back to Germany.

Soon after Erich had returned to Berlin, he had found a woman who could fulfil his short-term needs and little Karl was born nine months later. Erich had set up a lucrative underground business transporting disenfranchised youths from Berlin's Russian sector to safe houses in the American sector. Not only had he been able to make a handsome profit from the venture, but he had also managed to recruit these new West German citizens into his ever-expanding neo-Nazi army. He had spent years uniting Germany's disparate bands of neo-Nazi skinheads and loosely knit gangs of fascist thugs to form a formidable militia that would be ready to do his bidding at a moment's notice. Apart from regular training exercises, he kept his attack dogs primed and ready by sending them off to swell the ranks of right-wing street demonstrators, act as security guards for neo-Nazi meetings and serve as a ready reservoir for extremist agitators. He had provided his recruits with identity papers and had used his extensive assortment of contacts to get them jobs in the police and other powerful positions where they could one day further his cause.

Meanwhile, he had used his contacts at home and abroad to search for the missing car. He had no affinity with the white-supremacist rants of the American Nazi Party and their fourteen-word charter, but he accepted the organisation's help to scour North America for signs of the vanished vehicle. They reported regular sightings over the years and each one had to be investigated. Sommer had even less patience for the National Democratic Party of Germany, but its membership included many of his old Gestapo colleagues who shared his ideology. They were more than happy to allow Sommer to use their considerable resources to achieve his goals. He even found friends in the British Nationalist Party to help him search the United Kingdom. The Soviet Union and the Eastern Bloc were covered by his friends in the Stasi, the East German secret police. When his son, Karl, came of age, he joined the ranks of the Stasi and used his position to further his father's cause.

The Berlin Wall came down on November 9, 1989, and, with it, Erich's primary source of income. In a final act of defiance against the new world order, Erich died the following day, without fulfilling his sworn oath to the Deputy Führer. On his death bed, Karl made a similar oath and vowed not to rest until he found the documents that would restore Rudolf Hess's place in history.

Now the search was over—the time had come to retrieve the secret documents and shock the world with their contents.

As Ingrid finished clearing the table, the doorbell rang. She answered the door and allowed the two visitors to enter the house. One of them, a stocky skinhead in his early twenties, grabbed Karl Sommer's suitcase and hauled it outside. The other, a tall, handsome man with a scarred head, waited in the hallway.

Ingrid grabbed Sommer's coat and held it out for him as he made his way downstairs. 'You'll be off then, I suppose,' she said, draping the coat over her husband's back. 'Don't spare a thought for me, sitting alone awaiting your return.'

'That won't be necessary, my dear,' Sommer said as he straightened his coat. 'I won't be setting foot in this house again.' He nodded at the skinhead with the scarred head.

When the skinhead grabbed her, Ingrid let out an audible shriek as his hands cupped the sides of her head. He twisted her head until her neck cracked. Sommer gestured his approval as her body slumped to the floor.

Sommer spotted a photograph of his father with Hess in a silver frame on the mantelpiece. He picked it up and put it in his pocket. The skinhead opened the door and both men left the house without looking back. Sommer was pleased to see his men already assembled in the front yard to dispose of the body and move his belongings.

5

MARIA leaned back in the back seat of the limousine and allowed Luigi to free her breasts from the confines of her summer dress. He took her right nipple into his mouth and caressed it with his tongue. Goosebumps spread across Maria's flawless skin as Luigi bit down on the nipple ever so slightly. When it became erect and was hard to the touch, he took the whole areola into his mouth and sucked as if his life depended on it.

'The other one,' Maria whispered. 'Don't forget the other one.'

Luigi did as he was told and diverted his attention to the left breast. In size and texture, it was much the same as the right breast, but Maria appreciated the importance of balance. She squirmed on the velvet seat as Luigi's tongue darted in and out like a hungry iguana.

Maria liked Luigi but she didn't love him. She told him many times that she couldn't love a man who stole cars for a living. Being with Luigi was the highlight of her week but she didn't have the energy to disobey her mother on a regular basis. Appreciative as she was of his efforts to better himself by taking English lessons with Monsignor Marcus, it was clear he had no intention of severing his ties with the mafia.

Nothing good could come from falling in love with a criminal, her mother had always told her. If she was going to fall in love, it would be with a man like Monsignor Marcus. He would be the same as Marcus in every way, she thought, except he wouldn't be a priest. Besides, she was far too young to be worrying about love and wayward husbands. Life was too much fun to worry about such things.

Maria offered no resistance as Luigi slid her panties off and shifted his gaze downward. She parted her legs and watched as Luigi bowed his head and his tongue went to work on her once again. Varying his approach, he placed his hands on the seat on either side of her to speed up his tempo and rhythm. In the throes of ecstasy, she raised the arm rest on the left-hand side as the seat lifted slightly to the beat of Luigi's rhythm. Just then, she could have sworn she heard a clicking sound under her feet.

'What was that?' Maria asked.

'What was what?' Luigi lifted his head.

'Never mind. Keep doing what you were doing.'

'*Amore mio*, maybe now it's my turn?' Luigi said with a twinkle in his eye.

'Not yet, my love. I'll tell you when.'

Luigi frowned and resumed his position between her legs.

Marcus was walking along the second floor of the Pontifical Villas when something outside the window caught his eye. In the courtyard, he spotted what appeared to be a vintage Mercedes-Benz limousine in which two, possibly three, people were in flagrante.

'I don't believe it,' Marcus said under his breath as he scampered down the stairs.

Negotiating the steps like a seasoned steeplechaser, he kept his hand on the golden crucifix hanging around his neck to stop it from hitting him in the face. The Swiss Guard stationed at the main entrance managed to open the glass door just in time that Marcus didn't have to break his stride. When he reached the courtyard, he reluctantly broke into a run, being careful not to trip on his cassock. Despite the embarrassment he felt about running in public while wearing a cassock, Marcus was pleased he could exert himself without breaking a sweat. He had always been proud of his physical fitness, which he had honed as a younger man rowing *currachs* in Ireland.

Marcus was out of breath when he reached the vintage Mercedes-Benz. He looked a formidable sight in his priestly attire as he peered in through the back window. He could just about recognise Maria sitting in the back seat as Luigi fidgeted on the opposite seat.

The car park was nestled between the trees in the gardens to the west of the Papal apartments. It was guarded twenty-four hours a day by three security guards, who each worked an eight-hour shift. Space was limited and was reserved for long-time employees and residents of the Papal apartments. At the far end of the car park was a private garage that housed the Pope's bulletproof limousine, which had been used to transport him to and from Vatican City. But the limousine had become obsolete since the Pope acquired a helicopter. Marcus wondered how Luigi managed to convince the guard to let him park the Mercedes in such a reserved space—he assumed the boy must have invented some cock-and-bull story involving the Holy Father.

He waved his arm back and forth in a circular motion to direct Luigi to pull down the window. In the circumstances, he was reluctant to open the door in case he found Maria in a state of undress. Before he could object, Maria opened the back door and eased across the seat to make room for Marcus.

'It's a nice car, right enough,' Marcus said as he climbed into the back seat and reclined in the comfortable velvet seat. 'The question is: where did you get it?'

Luigi lowered his head and looked down at his feet for a moment. Then he looked up at Maria. 'I had no choice, Monsignor,' Luigi stammered. 'The Mountain knows where my mother lives.'

'The Mountain?'

'Yes, Silvio Montagna, the local capo. He makes me steal a car every time he gets an order from his clients. It's a small town—I can't avoid his soldiers forever.'

Marcus looked at Maria and noticed the perspiration on her skin. 'Maria, go back to my apartment and finish your work, like a good girl. I'll deal with you later.'

Marcus had no trouble believing Maria would break plenty of hearts as she eased her way into womanhood. She presented her left cheek to Luigi, who gave it the slightest of pecks, then she opened the door and jumped out of the car. As she closed the door and waved at Luigi, she looked as innocent and fragile as a child. Her small rounded breasts were accentuated by her floral summer dress, and her hazel hair, held back in a ponytail by a burgundy silk ribbon, took on a golden hue in the summer sun.

Luigi couldn't keep his eyes off her as she strolled across the car park.

'You like her very much, don't you?' Marcus said.

'Yes, Monsignor, but it's not easy. She makes my heart ache.'

'I feel the same way about Thai food.' Marcus laughed.

'When do we learn how to understand women, Monsignor?'

Marcus thought about that for a moment. 'I'm not so sure we're meant to understand them. Our inability to understand women is one of those things that make life worth living. The love of a good woman is man's greatest challenge in life. If we knew what they wanted, it would be easy to get them to love us. But where would be the fun in that?' Marcus fiddled with the door of the drinks cabinet in front of him and saw that it was empty and dusty. 'It would be like knowing how a good book ends before you finished reading it, or knowing the score of a football match before the final whistle was blown. I'm glad the path I have chosen in life does not require me to understand women. Understanding God is a much easier prospect.'

'Some days she appears to like me and other days she is angry.'

'In this instance, you should be more concerned about her mother.'

'Her mother?'

Signora Locatelli is a bad-tempered old crone with Sicilian blood. She works as a pastry chef in the kitchen and I wouldn't want to get on the wrong side of her.'

'I heard she once chopped off a finger of one of the Swiss Guards when he tried to take a slice of tiramisu.' Luigi squirmed in his seat.

'Imagine what she'll do if you do anything to hurt her only daughter.' Marcus placed his finger on his neck and made a slicing motion. He couldn't keep a straight face and erupted into a fit of laughter.

Luigi didn't see the funny side. 'Have you ever been in love with a woman?'

Marcus looked at Luigi without hesitation. 'Yes, for most of my life.'

'What do you mean? You're a monsignor.'

'I wasn't always a priest. I grew up on a small island where there was nothing to do but read books and play football. My best friend was beautiful and smart and all the boys liked her. But I was the only boy she liked. We were inseparable for most of our childhood, and then we went to university together. If I hadn't heard the calling to become a priest, I would have married her.'

'What happened to her?'

'She got pregnant while we were studying in Dublin. She returned home and I went to Rome to study for the priesthood.'

Luigi couldn't hide the look of surprise on his face.

'I know what you're thinking,' Marcus said, slapping the boy on the back of the head. 'I wasn't the father. We had never quite—' Marcus struggled to find the correct word, '*consummated* our feelings or even admitted that we were in love. And then she got drunk one night after exams, had a one-night stand with some *gurrier* from Dublin and became pregnant.'

'What's a *gurrier*?'

'A *gurrier* is someone like you, Luigi.' Marcus smiled. 'I returned home and helped her with her daughter, Lucy. She was a bit of a handful, like you. But we straightened her out.'

'Where is she now—the love of your life, I mean?'

'As a matter of fact, she's getting married to my best friend this week. Ain't that a kick in the head?'

Luigi didn't get the reference to the old song. 'What will I do about the car?'

Marcus held out his hand with the palm facing upward, prompting Luigi to hand over the keys. The priest rummaged through his own keys and absent-mindedly hooked the car key onto his own set of keys. 'Leave it to me,' said Marcus. 'I will have a word with The Mountain and set him straight on a few things. In the meantime, leave the car here and return to your gardening duties. It would be wise not to venture beyond the Apostolic boundary for a while.'

'What will you say to him? He doesn't listen to reason.'

'Maybe I'll send Signora Locatelli after him,' Marcus joked.

'You're not like any priest I've ever met, Monsignor.' Luigi opened the door and got out of the car.

'I'll take that as a compliment.' Marcus leaned forward as Luigi closed the door. 'By the way, how did you get the car in here in the first place?'

'I had this.' Luigi took an identification card out of his pocket and handed it over to Marcus. It appeared to be Father Salvatore's security pass, complete with his name and title; however, the photograph was clearly that of Luigi.

'Remind me to tighten security around here.'

'Yes, Monsignor.'

Marcus watched Luigi cross the yard and make his way to the villas. He was annoyed at the boy for slipping back into his old ways, but he was also angry at himself for allowing it to happen. No matter how Marcus looked at it, this was his fault. He was the director of Castel Gandolfo and he was responsible for security, especially when the

Pope was in residence. Luigi was also his responsibility and his decision to trust a serial car thief might have put the Pope in harm's way. But he decided he wasn't ready to give Luigi his marching orders; unfortunately, that meant seeking out Silvio Montagna to get him to leave the boy alone.

Marcus understood that the crime families enjoyed power and influence in Italian society but he also knew the Catholic Church was still a formidable force. He resolved to take a leaf out of Montagna's book. If 'The Mountain' was prepared to involve Luigi's mother, then Marcus would have a thing or two to say to Montagna's mother. Behind every mafioso thug was a mother who was religious and had supreme control. All Italian men listened to their mothers, Marcus reasoned, and all Italian mothers listened to their priests.

Marcus had never come across Montagna before but he had to respect his taste in cars. He admired the velvet seats and wooden panels because they reminded him of the confessional. Smiling to himself, he imagined travelling around the country using the back of the car as a sort of mobile confession box. He wondered if the Holy Father would like the idea.

Looking down on the floor of the car, he noticed a bulge under the carpet. It was unusual to see such an imperfection in a well-made German car. Reaching down to his feet, he pulled away a section of the carpet. He grabbed the elevated section of the wooden floorboard and could see what looked like a leather book hidden inside a concealed compartment. Picking up the book, he placed it on the seat beside him.

Marcus shivered when he made out the unmistakable symbol—the swastika—stamped into the leather. As far as he could make out, it was a journal of some sort, complete with a brass lock that kept it closed. He checked his pockets and cursed himself for forgetting to carry his Swiss Army knife. Using his keys, he tried each one to see if they would fit into the lock. No chance.

Gazing out the side window of the car, he considered the insanity of the situation. He was on Vatican property, sitting inside a stolen vintage limousine that used to belong to a Nazi, and he was holding an old diary that had been hidden inside the car since the war. An image of Hitler and the concentration camps flashed through his mind and he dropped the book on the floor in a knee-jerk reaction. He looked around to see if anyone was watching him. In the kiosk at the entrance to the car park, the security guard was reading a newspaper, oblivious to the existence of a stolen car on the car park he was supposed to be watching.

Marcus wondered what he should do. The car had to be moved so that Luigi couldn't be implicated in its theft and the Pope could be distanced from the whole sorry affair. The journal also had to be opened to ascertain its significance. Scanning the car park for anything out of the ordinary, he opened the back door and got out of the car. Opening the driver's side door, he climbed in and put his keys in the ignition. Marcus was just about to start the engine when he realised he was making a terrible mistake. The car was too conspicuous to be driven out in the open. Both the local mafia and the police were looking for it, and he would be pulled over as soon as he left the apostolic boundary. His mind was in a muddle.

Marcus got out of the car, grabbed the journal from the back seat and started walking. He had to clear his head and take a closer look at the Nazi book away from prying eyes, and he knew the perfect place where both tasks could be accomplished.

II

Doctor Dino Rugani consulted his notes when Mancuso walked into his autopsy chamber at the Questura Centrale in Piazza del Collegio Romano 3. In the centre of the room were two metal autopsy beds, one of which contained the body of the woman they had discovered at Tor Bella Monaca. Dino pulled away the white sheet that covered the body, revealing the incisions he had made during the autopsy.

'Several injuries to the face and head consistent with blows from a blunt instrument. Paint flecks suggest a tire lever or crowbar. Fairly new. The skull is fractured in two places.'

Dino moved around the corpse and pointed at a section of the skull. 'There and underneath.'

He took a closer look at the head and then returned to his notes. 'Death resulted from haemorrhaging of blood and cerebral edema. We've sent her dental records to the British Embassy, so you'll have a name in a day or two.'

'Any evidence of the attacker?' said Mancuso. 'Like blood or tissue?'

'There was blood under the fingernails, but not that of the victim.' Dino paused to let the detective sergeant take in the last piece of information. 'So, all you have to do is find out who it belongs to.'

Dino walked toward the chamber's exit and was just about to leave the room when he stopped. 'Oh, and there was hair on the clothing. Human and otherwise.'

'Otherwise? What do you mean by otherwise?'

'*Felis silvestris catus.*'
'What does that mean?'
'A cat.'

6

THE Gulfstream G-IV jet had seen better days, but it was still in good condition for a 20-year-old aircraft. The cabin was furnished with comfortable sofas and chairs, and the stylish lamps placed throughout provided discrete lighting. Consoles with computers, television monitors and all manner of communication devices were arranged along one side. Five technicians were busy operating the computer terminals and the satellite technology. The frantic tapping of their keyboards could be heard over the martial intensity of Wagner, which was playing on the sound system. Two stewardesses busied themselves running errands and catering to the passengers' every whim. But there was only one passenger who counted.

Karl Sommer stirred his tea and glowered at the crack on the china cup from which he was drinking. He was reminded of the opulence and optimism of National Socialism and lamented that even the Nazi movement had lost its glamour in times of austerity. He tapped his fingers in time with the music and remembered what the Führer had once said about the great composer: "In order to understand National Socialism, one first must understand Wagner."

The jet belonged to his private security company, which acted as a front for his more nefarious activities and allowed him to travel anywhere in the world without hindrance. It was always on standby at Berlin's Johannisthal Air Field and was equipped with state-of-the-art navigation computers and satellite technology.

'I have something, Herr Oberstleutnant,' said Heinz, one of the computer technicians.

Sommer was pleased to hear his men using the Stasi rank to which he had been elevated before the fall of East Germany's State Security Service. He looked at the large monitor hanging from the cabin ceiling on which the image from Heinz's computer was displayed.

'This is the Deputy Führer's car at Castel Gandolfo, about twenty kilometres south of Rome.' Heinz brought up an image of the Mercedes-Benz in the car park where Luigi had left it. 'I tracked the motorway cameras along the Autostrada Roma near the auto exhibition around the time of the theft and found the car travelling east. By jumping from one camera to another, I was able to follow the car onto the GRA ring road and the Appian Way as it headed south.'

'How long has it been there?' Sommer asked, unable to hide the beam of satisfaction on his face.

'The thief stole the car yesterday evening and arrived there just before dusk. If he had waited until nightfall, we would not have been able to track him. The car has been sitting there ever since.'

'Has anyone shown any interest in the car?'

'Yes, sir. Several people got in and out of the car since it has been there. One of those people was female. She spent some time in the car with a man, then another man joined them. They all got out and went off in different directions.'

Sommer thought about that for a moment. 'We have no time to waste. Where is the nearest airport?'

Heinz tapped a few keys on his computer and turned towards his leader. 'Aeroporto di Ciampino is just fifteen kilometres from Rome and ten from the car.'

'Very well, alert the pilot to land there. Have transport waiting when we arrive and tell our team on the ground to find that car.'

'Yes, sir.' Heinz rose from his chair and printed the coordinates of the private car park at Castel Gandolfo. 'One other thing, Herr Oberstleutnant.'

'What is it, Heinz?'

'Castel Gandolfo is the summer residence of the Pope.'

'Is the Pope in residence?'

'Yes, sir.'

'What level of security do they have on the ground?'

'The Swiss Guards appear to be concentrating their efforts along the perimeter and the interior of the Papal Palace. The car park is monitored by an outside security firm and is guarded by one man.'

'That seems like a sensible place to hide a car for a day or two,' Sommer said. 'The security guard must be in on it. The thieves must have lined up a buyer for the car before they stole it. Nobody in their right mind would steal such a car unless they knew they could sell it. We better act fast before they move the car again.'

'We're on that, Herr Oberstleutnant,' said another technician. 'Our operatives on the ground have their orders.'

Sommer smiled as he leaned back in his leather seat and admired the curvaceous legs of the blonde stewardess who was refilling his teacup. He raised his hand and gestured for her to sit in the chair beside him. When she was comfortable, Sommer undid the buttons of her blouse and placed his hand inside her bra. He squeezed her breast and gazed into her eyes, smiling as her expression changed from arousal to pain.

After some heated negotiations, the Gulfstream was authorised to land at Aeroporto di Ciampino. Even though he'd arrived on a private jet, Sommer and his entourage had to go through the main terminal building and passport control like everyone else.

Dressed in a cream-coloured linen suit, white shirt and dark tie, Sommer looked at least ten years younger than his sixty-two years. His fair hair was closely cropped and matched his neatly groomed goatee. At one point six metres, he was shorter than his companions but what he lacked in height, he more than made up for in confidence and charisma. He was greeted by three neo-Nazi skinheads wearing expensive suits. They attempted to give him the Nazi salute, but Sommer stopped them just in time. One of them, Heinrich, took a step forward.

'We don't want to make spectacles of ourselves,' Sommer chastised him. 'We are trying to remain inconspicuous, after all.'

'I trust you had a pleasant flight, *mein kommandant*,' Heinrich said in German.

'We will communicate only in English from now on. Take me to the car and tell me about the situation.'

On the way to the car park, Heinrich filled Sommer in on what they had done in the past several hours and the preparations they had made for his arrival. They walked through the VIP car park and stopped when they reached a fleet of silver Mercedes-Benz S-Class saloons. Heinrich opened the door of the first car for Sommer and then he jumped in beside his leader. 'I have sent a team to Castel Gandolfo to take the car. They have been told about the secret compartment. But we have to be careful—security is bound to be beefed up while the Pope is in residence.'

Sommer raised an eyebrow and looked at Heinrich. 'Let's not be too careful. We have to retrieve those documents and I don't care what we have to do to make that happen.'

Heinrich looked anxious as he shifted in his seat. 'Can you give us a little more information, Herr Oberstleutnant? It might help us if we knew what we are looking for.'

'All in good time—I will address the team when we reach our base.'

The convoy of silver Mercedes wended its way through the streets surrounding the airport. When they reached the entrance to a private airplane hangar, they entered the building one by one, and the huge doors were closed behind them.

'The Gulfstream will be brought over as soon as it clears customs,' said Heinrich.

'Do we know the identity of the thief?' Sommer asked.

'Yes, sir. His name is Luigi Manetti. He is a gardener at Castel Gandolfo's Barberini Gardens. He also appears to be a minor associate of the Gallico di Palmi crime family. We believe it was this crime family that instructed him to steal the car.'

Sommer opened the door of the car and surveyed the scene. 'How organised is this crime family?'

'They have an army of about two hundred men,' said Heinrich. 'And, of course, the local police are paid to turn a blind eye to their activities.'

'I didn't come this far to be outwitted by a bunch of lazy Italians.'

A small army of neo-Nazi skinheads was standing to attention in formation when Sommer got out of the car. The skinheads greeted him with the 'Heil Hitler' salute when he turned and faced them.

Sommer returned the salute and cleared his throat. 'For more than half a century, Reich Minister Rudolf Hess has been portrayed as a madman—a naive simpleton who ruined his life on a fool's errand.' He didn't need a microphone—his voice echoed across the airplane hangar as the words came thundering out of his mouth. 'The journal that now eludes us reveals the true purpose of the Reich Minister's flight to Scotland in 1941. It proves that the Führer sent Hess to make peace with Great Britain. It also confirms that the Allies rejected Germany's hand of friendship and opted instead to prolong a war that destroyed millions of lives.'

He paced the floor in front of his men and watched with pride as they hung on his every word. 'When Hess landed in Scotland, he never made it to a scheduled meeting with the King's brother, Prince George, the Duke of Kent. He was captured by the British, discredited and forced to undergo the indignity of the Nuremberg War Trials.'

Sommer grabbed a glass that was resting on a nearby table and drank some water. 'He was convicted of committing crimes against humanity during a conflict in which he played no part. Despite his attempts to stop the war, he was imprisoned along with all the other Nazi leaders. He spent the rest of his life locked up like an animal in Spandau Prison in West Berlin, where he was assassinated by British agents in 1987. Before he left for Scotland, he hid the journal in a secret compartment in the car that we now seek. My father had always intended to find a safer hiding place, but the Führer arrested him and the rest of Hess's staff soon after the Reich Minister was captured. By the time my father was released, the car had disappeared. He and I have spent the past sixty years searching for it.'

Sommer stared into the distance as his army listened. 'The journal contains a letter written by Hitler explaining Hess's actions. I never read the letter in question, but Reich Minister Hess explained its contents to my father. In it, Hitler commends Hess for his brave actions and assures him the world will know he fulfilled his destiny by bringing peace to all nations. I am the only person alive who knows the secret compartment in which these documents are hidden and how to access it. The Reich Minister never got a chance to fulfil his destiny—he was robbed of the opportunity to take his rightful place in history. My father failed him and, to my eternal shame, I have failed him. Our mission is to find that journal and show the world that Reich Minister Rudolf Hess was a true hero.'

He raised his clenched fist into the air. 'Drastic measures are required. We must find this car and its hidden documents, and put an end to this matter once and for all.' He raised his arm in a Nazi salute and shouted, 'Heil Hitler.' His army responded with the same salute and, while Sommer looked on with pride, they repeated the term 'Heil Hitler' more than a dozen times.

Heinrich ordered the men to get on with their work as he guided Sommer to a lounge area along the east wall of the hangar. The lounge contained a sofa, armchairs, a coffee table and a widescreen television, all arranged over a large Persian rug. To the side was an office with a desk, a computer and a telephone. Heinrich walked over to the drinks cabinet next to the office and poured a glass of peach schnapps, Sommer's favourite drink. He brought the drink to Sommer, who was already sitting in an armchair in the lounge. Sommer switched on the television and pressed several buttons on the remote control until an image of the carpark at Castel Gandolfo came into view. 'Two of our operatives are wearing cameras mounted to headpieces. We can see everything they see.'

Sommer watched as his operatives made their way through the narrow streets of Castel Gandolfo and headed for their target.

7

THE security guard walked out of his kiosk when the two silver S-Class Mercedes-Benz saloons pulled up outside the gates of the private car park at Castel Gandolfo. He smiled as he approached the driver's door and got ready to perform his favourite part of the job. Informing motorists that they were not authorised to access the car park gave him power he did not possess in other aspects of his life. When he had an opportunity to exert such authority, he grabbed it with gusto. But before he could order them to back away from the entrance, a man in the back seat of the lead car lowered his window, pointed his silenced pistol at the guard's head and shot him between the eyes.

Two skinheads got out of the lead car and opened the boot. They picked up the dead security guard and dumped him inside. One of the men was dressed in an expensive Armani suit while the other was wearing the full regalia of the Swiss Guard. Both were wearing micro cameras on their clothes.

The men walked across the car park towards the vintage limousine, followed by the two cars. The skinhead in the Swiss Guard uniform approached the limousine and opened the back door. The gaping hole in the middle of the floor was the first thing he saw, and the plush carpet rolled across the floor to reveal the secret compartment. Reaching his hand into the compartment, he confirmed it was empty. Easing himself off the back seat, he closed the back door and opened the driver's side door. After conducting a cursory examination of the front seat to see if anything was out of place, he was surprised to see the key still in the ignition. He took out the key and looked at the key fob to which it was attached. It said, 'Apartment 2A'. Separating the car key from the rest of the keys on the keyring, he placed it back in the ignition. After taking another look around the interior, he got out and approached his Armani-suited colleague. 'Drive her back to the hangar and make sure you are not followed.'

The driver nodded, started the engine and drove the car out the main gates. The four occupants of the second silver Mercedes, all of whom were wearing the uniform of the Swiss Guard, stayed in their car and awaited further instructions.

At the airplane hangar, Sommer was consumed with rage as he watched events unfold on his monitors. He finished his schnapps and threw his glass at the television. The glass missed the television by some distance and hit a picture of Marlene Dietrich on the wall behind it. Turning to Heinrich, he shouted. 'What is the meaning of this? Where are the fucking documents? Nobody knew about that compartment but me.'

Heinrich took out his cell phone and called one of the operatives at the car park.

Sommer had waited for this moment his entire life and felt no closer to finding the documents. It was inconceivable to him that someone else could have found them. 'Find Apartment 2A,' He shouted. 'Get a car ready. I want to go over there.'

Heinrich relayed the instructions over the phone. When he was finished, he turned to Sommer. 'It is not a good idea for you to go there, Herr Oberstleutnant. The area is guarded by highly trained soldiers and my operatives can handle the situation. They are dressed as Swiss Guards and they can get in and out with a minimum of fuss. The Reich Minister's car will be here soon. We can examine it and figure out our next move.'

'We're wasting time,' Sommer barked. 'Whoever stole the car must have stumbled upon the secret compartment. We must find him.'

Less than half an hour later, the huge doors of the airplane hangar slid open and in rolled the vintage limousine. Sommer rose from his armchair and clapped eyes on the car for the first time. It looked the same as his father had described it, right down to the gleaming bumpers, which shined as bright as they did on that fateful day when Hess travelled to the air base in Augsburg. Opening the back door, he checked under the carpet, under the back seats and all over the back of the car, but he could find no sign of the documents. He opened the boot and searched every inch, but to no avail. One of the men crawled under the car and began checking the undercarriage. Sommer returned to the lounge area and monitored the television footage. He watched as the five remaining operatives made their way across the car park towards the Papal Palace.

II

Marcus was deep in thought when he entered O'Reilly's Irish Pub. He made a beeline for his usual stool at the counter and caught the eye of the bartender. 'A pint please, Brian.'

The bartender grabbed a glass and started pouring. 'Coming up.'

Like every other Irish pub around the world, the interior consisted of dark wood and brass fittings. The walls were decorated with framed pictures of Irish writers, poets, sporting heroes and revolutionaries, and the wooden floor was covered in sawdust. The music of Christy Moore played in the background, and the Sacred Heart of Jesus took pride of place above the front door, alongside pictures of John F. Kennedy and the Pope. Except for the smell of Italian coffee percolating behind the counter, the pub had a distinctive Irish atmosphere. A small widescreen television was nestled in the corner, but it was only switched on during sporting events.

Very few people knew that O'Reilly's was owned by Marcus. Everyone considered Eamon the manager, but it was really Marcus who called the shots. Because of his position in the Church, Marcus preferred to keep his ownership a secret. Even so, he enjoyed observing the day-to-day workings of the pub without the staff or the punters knowing who he was. If he noticed any aspect of the business that needed to be improved, he told Eamon and nobody was any the wiser.

When Marcus had returned to Italy with his father in tow, it made sense to get Eamon some sort of job to keep him active and out of trouble while Marcus resumed his career in Vatican City. An Irish pub had seemed like the perfect venture since the old man had spent so much of his life in pubs.

As it turned out, Marcus and Eamon were the pub's best customers, not only because they enjoyed the gaiety and banter of the local Irish community but also because it reminded them of home. The Pope would likely take a dim view of his extracurricular activities, so he was careful to be as discreet as possible. Of course, discretion wasn't one of Eamon's qualities, which meant Marcus had to be discreet for both of them.

Apart from himself and Brian, the pub was empty. Brian placed the pint of Guinness on the counter and they both watched as the creamy froth settled into blackness. Marcus had gone to a lot of trouble to make sure his pub served the best pint of Guinness in Italy: barrels of Guinness were sent over from Dublin every month and all the staff was trained in the art of pouring it.

Marcus spotted a copy of the *Corriera della Sera* at the end of the bar. He grabbed it and was shocked to see a picture of Luigi's vintage limousine on the front page. The picture was accompanied by an article on the car theft the previous evening.

'It's amazing what people can get away with these days,' Brian said, pointing at the newspaper.

'Isn't that the truth.' Marcus waited for Brian to turn his attention to dusting the liquor bottles before he placed the Nazi journal on the counter, careful to hide the swastika. Grabbing a steak knife from behind the counter, he picked up the journal and inserted the tip of the knife into the lock. No amount of jiggling would open the lock and he cursed as he increased the pressure.

Finally, he heard a satisfying click.

Holding his breath, the priest undid the clasp and opened the journal. He shuffled through the pages and was disappointed to find the entire thing was written in German. Some of the words were recognisable: Duke of Hamilton, Winston Churchill, King George VI, Duke of Kent, Joseph Kennedy. Marcus recognised the flight plans and drawings of a World War II fighter plane. As he turned the pages, he came across a folded sheet of paper that looked like a letter. The red wax swastika seal had been broken and the paper had yellowed with age. A cursory glance at the reverse confirmed that it was a letter. Marcus gasped and looked around to make sure nobody was watching before he took a sip of his pint and returned his attention to the letter. It was addressed to Deputy Führer Rudolf Hess. Marcus opened the letter, scanned the German text and couldn't believe his eyes when he reached the end of the document. The signature at the bottom of the page was unmistakable. It was signed by Adolf Hitler. Marcus folded the letter and placed it in the inside pocket of his cassock. Beads of sweat rolled down his face as he considered the consequences of what he had just seen. He felt like a helpless animal who had just stumbled onto a nest of vipers.

Someone will be looking for this document, he thought. Luigi had stolen the car and the theft was all over the news. His initial reaction was to hand it over to the Holy See for safe keeping, but then he decided it might not be wise to involve the Vatican. It was too late for that—the Vatican was already involved. The car was parked on the Papal Palace grounds, which were owned by the Vatican. He didn't have to understand the contents of the letter or the journal to know they were both bad news. The fact that the letter was written by Hitler was significant enough, but what if it contained some important information? The letter would have to be translated before he could make any sense of it. And he knew of only one person who could translate the documents and explain their significance. Marcus sighed—he would have to get in touch with his friend Willie sooner than expected.

Two people walked into the pub, a man and woman, but they paid no attention to Marcus as they made their way to the other end of the counter. Marcus waited for Brian to serve them before he leaned over the counter and looked around for somewhere to hide the journal. He found a cigar box full of old fishing hooks and grabbed it. Emptying the hooks on the countertop, he blew into the box to get rid of the remaining dust and debris. Checking to make sure it was the right size, he placed the journal inside the box and closed the lid. Wrapping a thick elastic band around the box, he took another sip of his drink and considered his options.

Marcus's thoughts were interrupted by the sound of Brian cleaning the bottles in the whiskey display case behind the counter. He looked at the cigar box and then at the display case.

'Any chance you could throw this behind those bottles, like a good man?' Marcus said, handing the cigar box to Brian.

The bartender looked at the box and did as he was told. 'That's a nice box. I have one just like it for my fly hook collection.' Marcus coughed and placed the newspaper on top of the fly hooks. He grabbed his pint and tried not to go red in the face.

Where better to keep it safe, Marcus thought? *Nobody would look for it in here and Brian has probably already forgotten about it.*

'Can I use the back office?' Marcus asked.

The office was out of bounds to customers, but all the staff members had been instructed that Marcus was the exception to the rule. The priest was prepared to go over Brian's head and call Eamon, but he didn't want to make waves. He hoped he could do what needed to be done as quietly as possible.

'I don't see why not.'

Marcus finished his Guinness and walked over to the end of the bar. Pulling up the counter, he went through to the office and looked around. The computer was already switched on and connected to the Internet, so he sat down and switched on the scanner.

Picking up the phone on the desk, he dialled a number and waited for his friend to answer. 'How's it going there, your lordship?'

'Ah, Marcus my boy,' said the voice on the other end. 'What a sound for sore ears. I hope you're not calling to cancel the wedding.'

Willie Shuttleworth-Banks was not a lord, but Marcus liked to tease him because of his posh English accent. They had been friends and business partners in Ireland, and Marcus knew he could trust him with his life. Willie had retired to Italy some years before and they had kept in contact.

'Not a chance,' said Marcus. 'But I can't stay on long. Do you mind if I email you a German document for translation? You're not going to believe it when you see it. I have a few loose ends to tie up and then I'll head down there to discuss it with you. I'll be there in plenty of time for the wedding, don't worry.'

Marcus didn't see any point in telling Willie the whole story over the phone—partly because he didn't know the whole story and partly because he didn't want to upset his friend in the run-up to the wedding.

'No problem, dear fellow. I look forward to seeing you.'

Marcus disconnected the call and put the phone down. Looking around to make sure Brian wasn't in the vicinity, he reached into his pocket and took out the letter. Placing it in the scanner, he grabbed the computer mouse and got to work.

After several orchestrated taps on the keyboard, the job was done. He attached the scanned document to the email and sent it to Willie. Careful to delete both the scanned image and the sent email, he retrieved the letter from the scanner. When everything was done, he logged out of his email account and switched off the computer. Marcus was about to get out of the chair when he spotted an unused manila envelope and a pile of postage stamps on the desk. He placed the Hitler letter inside the manila envelope and then licked the stamps one by one before arranging them on the top right corner. He licked the flap, sealed the envelope and wrote Willie's address on the outside.

A small crowd had appeared in the pub when Marcus returned from the office. Day-trippers from Rome, he thought as he made his way towards the door. He made a mental note to employ more waiting staff during the day for just such an occurrence. Marcus would have liked to stay and help Brian with the customers, but he didn't want to blow his cover. Besides, he had to get back to his apartment and collect a few things before heading south to join Willie in Sperlonga.

On his way out the door, he spotted a letter box on the sidewalk. He dropped the Hitler letter into the box and hoped it would reach Willie safely. A plan was forming in Marcus's head that involved driving the stolen limousine to Sperlonga in the cover of night. The first thing he would have to do was move the car from its current location and lay low until it got dark. Then he would make his way to seaside resort and find somewhere to hide the vehicle. He rummaged through his pockets for his keys, but he couldn't find them. Panic was about to set in as he stopped in his tracks and tried to retrace his movements. Then he remembered—he left the keys in the limousine. Running as fast as he could, he bolted across Strada Statale and made for the shortcut through the pontifical gardens.

8

A S MARCUS made his way across the Barberini Gardens, taking in the aromas as he passed through the square of holly oaks, the paths of roses and aromatic herbs, and the magnolia garden. His gaze wandered towards the ancient Roman ruins that were built during the time of Emperor Domitian. A contingent of Swiss Guards came into view as the path veered east and the glow of the sun hit him in the face. He was surprised to see the Holy Father, surrounded by guards, sitting on a bench in the magnolia garden. Marcus had forgotten that the Pope liked to wander the gardens and take in the stunning view over Lake Albano. Trying to cross the adjacent path unnoticed, he sighed when the eagle-eyed pontiff beckoned him over. Marcus smiled as he approached the Holy Father, kneeled before him and kissed the ring. No matter how much of a hurry he was in, it didn't do to insult the Pope by giving him a wide berth.

'Where are you off to in such a hurry?' the Pope inquired.

'Ah, you know yourself, Holy Father—things to do, people to see.'

'You should take the time to enjoy the magnificent flora and aromas, young man.'

'I should, Holy Father. The garden is beautiful this time of year.'

The Pope looked at Marcus with a quizzical look on his face. 'What are you up to, my boy? I can always tell when you're keeping something from me.'

'I don't know what you mean, Holy Father.'

'You needn't think you're pulling the wool over my eyes—I know all about your father's little business venture across the road.' The Pope looked at Marcus with a mischievous twinkle in his eye. 'But there's something else, isn't there?'

Marcus was relieved the Pope did not yet seem to be aware of the stolen Nazi limousine in the car park. 'There are no flies on you, Holy Father.'

'I must find the time to go over there myself and try some of your famous Connemara poteen.'

Marcus tried not to look embarrassed. The sheer magnitude of the Holy Father's wealth of information never ceased to amaze him. He must have spies in every corner of the globe—but they still have no idea about the limousine.

'Your father told me about the forthcoming wedding,' the Pope said. 'Are you looking forward to it?'

'Looking forward' was probably too optimistic a term for what he was feeling about the upcoming nuptials. The truth was that Marcus had conflicting emotions about the wedding, and he suspected the event would force him to confront his personal demons. After all, Sarah had been the love of his life, once upon a time, and Willie was his best friend. He was happy for them, but he reserved the right to resent them with equal measure. This resentment may have discouraged from offering the happy couple the services of the Vatican for their special day. It wouldn't have been difficult to ask the Pope to marry his friends and to make the Sistine Chapel available for the occasion. Instead, he remained distant and inaccessible, and he feared he would never be able to forgive himself for that.

'Yes, Holy Father.'

Of course, his apprehension about the wedding had been put into perspective by recent developments. He was brought back to the present by the sound of police sirens.

Both men turned their heads towards the Pontifical Villas as the sirens grew louder. The Swiss Guards raised their hands to their earpieces in unison as instructions were received from their superiors. Marcus got up to investigate but his path was blocked by one of the guards. 'Please wait here for a moment, Monsignor.'

Marcus sat back down next to the Pope, who put a reassuring hand on his knee. 'Relax, my son. I'm sure it's nothing.'

Marcus stared off into the distance and felt as if the weight of the world were on his shoulders. He had no way of knowing what was coming next, but he was sure it would have a lot to do with a stolen car and a Nazi manuscript. His world was about to come crashing down around his head and he wished he could confide in the man sitting next to him. Just then, a battalion of Swiss Guards descended on them. They surrounded the Pope and whisked him away, his feet hardly touching the ground as he was ushered to safety. One of the soldiers waited behind to escort Marcus back to his apartment.

'What's going on?' Marcus asked the soldier.

'The Papal Villas have been breached; we are taking the Holy Father back to Rome.'

II

As his partner droned on about the boundaries of jurisdiction imposed by the Swiss Guard, Detective Sergeant Mancuso couldn't keep his eyes off the message that was scrawled on the bedroom wall. It appeared to be written in blood and there was a lot of it. It was signed with a red swastika that gave him the creeps. It said: *If you want your friends back, call this number – 06 577 8418.*

'All the apartments here on this wing are used by Vatican employees and priests,' said Detective Rossi. 'This apartment is used by Monsignor Marcus Nee.'

The two detectives were standing in what looked like the smaller of the apartment's two bedrooms.

'What are we doing here?' asked Mancuso, who continued to stare at the message.

'At the very least, we're looking at a kidnapping,' said Rossi.

'Yes, but how many people?'

'That's the strange thing.' Rossi consulted his notes. 'We found three clean prints, not including those of the monsignor. You'll never guess who one of those prints belonged to?'

'Surprise me.'

'Luigi Manetti.'

'The plot thickens,' said Mancuso. 'His name is coming up a lot. What the fuck is a minor mafioso malcontent doing at the home of a Catholic monsignor with the ear of the Pope? And where is the vintage Mercedes he stole?'

'We don't have the results of that red stuff yet, but I'd bet a week's wages it's not human blood,' said Rossi.

Mancuso pried himself away from the message on the wall to have a better look around the room. He lifted the bed and turned it on its side. On the floor, next to the wall, was a tin of red paint with a large piece of cloth hanging out of it.

'Remind me not to bet with you.' Mancuso walked out into the hallway and watched as the forensic team went about its business.

When Marcus returned to his apartment, he was overwhelmed by the devastation he saw. A crowd of police and forensic officials was sifting through the rooms, gathering evidence and trying to make some sense out of what had happened there. A contingent of Swiss Guards was congregating in the hallway and they didn't look best pleased.

Marcus had already noted that the vintage limousine was no longer in the car park where he had left it. It didn't take a genius to figure out that the people who stole the car used his keys to enter his apartment. Marcus walked in through the open door and surveyed the scene: the décor had been reduced to tattered bits of fabrics and wallpaper; the television had been turned upside down and all the furniture had been smashed; and the glass frame holding his Papal letter of appointment signed by the Holy Father had been thrown to the floor and broken. The police seemed not to notice him as he meandered about. He walked into his bedroom and saw that his bed had been turned upside down and the pictures on the wall had been knocked down. To his eternal shame, his father's collection of *Playboy* magazines was strewn across the floor for all to see. One of the Swiss Guards eyed him with what Marcus supposed was a look of disdain.

He went across the hallway to Eamon's room and could not hide his fury at the chaos he saw before him. If he hadn't realised the implications of the Nazi journal before, he was now aware. And three innocents, including his father, were in harm's way because of his discovery. He took a firm hold of the door to stop himself from collapsing. His eyes focused on the swastika and he cursed himself for allowing evil to visit such a holy place. He entered the kitchen and saw the same turmoil. All the food from the shelves had been emptied onto the floor and the plates and cups had been destroyed. He touched the kettle and jumped when it scolded him. Whatever had happened, it'd happened recently. He didn't notice the heavy-set man sitting at the kitchen table looking at him.

The man smiled and offered Marcus a seat. 'My name is Detective Sergeant Scott Mancuso from Interpol. And you are Monsignor Marcus Nee, I suspect?'

'Yes, that's correct.' Marcus sat.

'I hear you are the Pope's favourite—his protégé, so to speak.'

'I wouldn't know about that.'

'The break-in seems to be limited to your apartment. How many people live here with you? Who are the "friends" referred to in the message?'

'I live here with my father, Eamon. My housekeeper, Maria, who was working here today, and one of our gardeners, Luigi, may have been here as well.'

'That's quite a party,' Mancuso said. 'What would the Nazis want with them?'

Before Marcus could answer, they were joined by Rossi.

'This is Giovanni Rossi, special liaison between Interpol and the Carabinieri.'

Rossi smiled at Marcus and then gestured for Mancuso to join him in the living room. When they were out of earshot, Rossi handed his partner a sheet of paper. 'There's supposed to be a security guard posted in the private car park but he hasn't been seen in hours. Can we assume his disappearance is the handiwork of either the Mafiosi or the neo-Nazis?' Rossi offered.

'We can't assume anything, you know that,' said Mancuso. 'But it's a fair bet.'

'What do they all want with the monsignor?'

'That goddamned car must have something to do with this,' Mancuso said. 'I'll bet Luigi parked the car here and whoever kidnapped those people took it. See what you can get from our friends at the Ministry of the Interior.'

Mancuso frowned when he saw Jessica Barkman enter the apartment. She made a bee-line for the kitchen, where she must have caught a glimpse of Marcus. The detective sergeant scampered across the apartment to block her path and ushered her into the spare bedroom, where the message was scrawled on the wall. 'How did you get here so quickly? I've only just figured out that this crime scene might be connected to your missing Mercedes.'

'The police chief thought you might forget to tell me, so he called me with the news.'

'I don't believe you.'

'Now that I'm here, detective, you might as well let me look around.'

'That's detective *sergeant*. Suppose you tell me what's so goddamned important about that car, apart from its obvious historical significance.'

'I could tell you, but then I'd have to kill you.'

Mancuso did not try to suppress the look of annoyance on his face.

'Okay,' said Jessica. 'I'll tell you if you let me sit in on your interview with the monsignor.'

'Nice try, lady. I haven't interviewed him myself yet.' Mancuso looked irritated when Rossi joined them.

Rossi looked at Jessica and smiled. 'The Brits have been giving us the run-around on the identity of our Jane Doe—something to do with a bank holiday. It'll probably be next week before we get anything.' Rossi handed Mancuso a file as he walked away.

Mancuso eyed Jessica. 'Did you find out anything about our murdered Brit, like you promised?'

'Not a lot,' said Jessica. 'Like the man said, it's a bank holiday.'

'Okay, I'll let you see the priest if you tell us what's so important about the car and if you run these prints and dental records through your system at the consulate.'

'It's a deal,' she said, taking the file from Mancuso.

Jessica cleared her throat and leaned toward Mancuso, as if to reveal a secret that only he could hear. 'The car contains secret documents that Her Majesty's government would very much like to recover.'

'What secret documents?'

'I can't tell you that, detective sergeant. Suffice it to say that we have permission from the Italian Ministry of Foreign Affairs to recover the documents at all costs.'

'What makes you think the car contains documents?'

'According to my contacts at Six, the documents would be very embarrassing for the British royal family if they got out,' Jessica said.

'How do you know all this? What makes you think these documents even exist?'

'Karlheinz Pintsch, Hess's adjutant, confirmed the existence of the documents when he was debriefed after the war. He confirmed that they were hidden in a secret compartment in the car. We also questioned Hess's driver, Erich Sommer, when the Russians let him go in 1955. He didn't reveal much beyond the fact that the documents include a letter written by Hitler.'

'That doesn't explain why Rome's nastiest crime family is in cahoots with neo-Nazi skinheads?

'That's why we must interview the monsignor,' said Jessica, who was already on her way to the kitchen.

'I will interview the monsignor, while you sit quietly.'

When they reached the kitchen, Marcus was sitting at the table drinking coffee.

'I see you've helped yourself to refreshments,' said Mancuso, pulling out a chair.

'Well, it is my kitchen,' said Marcus.

'This is a crime scene,' Mancuso corrected. 'You're not supposed to touch anything.'

'This is Vatican territory and, as such, I enjoy diplomatic coffee-drinking privileges.'

Mancuso smiled and looked at Jessica. 'This is Jessica Barkman from the British Embassy. She will sit in on our formal interview.'

'Informal interview,' Marcus corrected. 'You're forgetting my diplomatic immunity.'

'Okay, shall we start?' Mancuso asked.

Marcus nodded.

'Your gardener Luigi, who seems to have the run of the apartment, is a known car thief with connections to the Mafia. As a matter of fact, he stole a car yesterday.' Mancuso waited for Marcus to respond. 'This is when you respond,' Mancuso said.

'I didn't hear you ask a question.'

'Are you in the habit of entertaining Mafiosi scumbags at your home, monsignor?'

'I reject the premise of the question,' Marcus offered. 'In the first place, I wasn't entertaining him—I was teaching him English. In the second, Luigi is a petty thief who is trying to turn over a new leaf—he's hardly a maniacal warlord.'

'Do you know anything about a stolen Mercedes-Benz limousine?'

'As a matter of fact, I do. Luigi parked the blasted thing in our private car park this morning. I was very cross with him but he promised not to do it again.'

'Was he acting alone?' Mancuso asked.

'He was coerced into stealing the car by Silvio Montagna, the local capo of the Gallico di Palmi family. The poor lad has been trying to go straight for ages but they threatened his mother. I have a good mind to seek out Montagna's mother and see what she thinks of her son's shenanigans.'

'Wouldn't it be great if all we had to do to stop the scumbags was to have a talk with their mothers? Mancuso joked. When he didn't get a laugh, he added, 'What about the neo-Nazis?'

'What about them?' Marcus asked.

'Why are they writing messages on your wall?'

Marcus wanted to help the police as much as possible, but he had to be careful about revealing too much. He was sure Hitler's letter was the key to getting his father back. He would tell the police about the journal in good time, but Hitler's letter was a gem he would have to hold on to until it was most needed. 'I don't know. We'll have to call the number to find out, I suppose. I'm a bit anxious about my father—and the other two, of course.'

'We'll have to get some more information before we can do that.'

'Did you see the car, monsignor?' Jessica asked.

'Yes. Luigi brought it here to show my housekeeper, Maria.'

'Did you or Luigi find any documents hidden inside the car?' Jessica asked.

'No.'

Nobody spoke for a moment. Marcus shifted in his chair and tried not to let the prolonged silence make him paranoid.

'As the director of this place, you are in charge of car park security, isn't that correct?' Mancuso asked.

'Yes,' said Marcus. 'We hire a private security firm to guard the car park and the gardens. The Swiss Guard protect everything else.'

'So, there's a guard posted at the car park, right?'

'Yes. The car park is guarded twenty-four hours.'

'Well, the guard is missing now,' Mancuso said, 'so we can assume whoever took your friends also took the guard.'

'There's no security in this wing of the Papal Palace. Anyone can come and go unnoticed,' said Marcus.

'Look, there's something you're not telling us,' Jessica said, sounding frustrated. 'If it weren't for the message scrawled across the bedroom wall, we could assume Luigi did this. Or maybe his mafioso friends. As things stand, we have to blame the neo-Nazis. But why didn't they just take the car and leave? Why did they have to come up here? You must have something else they want.'

'You better start helping us out here, Monsignor Nee,' said Mancuso. 'You have a known car thief connected to the Mafia in your apartment, a missing security guard and a specific message from a bunch of Nazis.' He leaned over the table and continued in a more conciliatory tone. 'You found something in the car, didn't you? Something those assholes want badly.' The police officer looked in Jessica's direction. 'Well, they're not the only ones looking for those documents.'

'If you give us the documents, we can find your father and the other two,' said Jessica, who stood up from her chair and started pacing the kitchen. She looked at Mancuso, who seemed irritated at her interrogation strategy. 'I wonder if I could speak with Monsignor Nee in private, detective sergeant?'

Mancuso sighed and rose from his chair. He gestured to Rossi to follow him out.

9

ESPITE the occasional breeze coming from the open doors and windows, the airplane hangar was hot and clammy. The space was so big it could accommodate three or four mid-sized jumbo jets. The Gulfstream was parked to one side of the hangar along with several Mercedes saloons. The vintage Mercedes limousine was also parked there but it looked nothing like it did in the museum; the seats and all the luxurious upholstery had been ripped out and all that was left of the interior was a metal shell. The wheels had also been taken off and the car was left resting on four blocks of wood.

Sommer's neo-Nazi soldiers had made themselves at home since arriving at the airplane hangar; they'd set up an electric barbecue in the far corner and a makeshift kitchen where they prepared salads and cooked savoury meatballs, wiener schnitzel and several varieties of German sausages. When they weren't eating, the soldiers went about their duties as they awaited fresh orders. The computer technicians worked on a bank of computers that had been laid out near the lounge area. More than a dozen of the men had been stationed outside the hangar and in the vicinity to deal with uninvited guests. The music of Wagner played in the background as Sommer listened.

In the middle of the floor were three wooden chairs, on which Eamon, Luigi and Maria were tied. Their hands and legs were bound with rope and their mouths were gagged with pieces of cloth. Maria seemed the least comfortable of the three and she made whimpering sounds that were barely audible over the music.

Sommer stood in front of Maria and poked her breasts with the end of his walking stick. His cruelty prompted an instant reaction from Luigi, who squirmed and cried as he struggled to come to Maria's aid. Eamon tried to speak but the gag in his mouth limited his contribution to a few muffled whines.

'You know, my dear, my father was tortured by the Russians for five years. They broke all his fingers and, when he wouldn't break, they scooped his left eye out of his head and fed it to one of his comrades. They kept him in a dark room for months on end with no one to keep him company but the rats and the cockroaches.'

Eamon struggled in his chair as Maria's whimpering became louder.

'What he wouldn't have given for a little Wagner during his incarceration.'

Maria shook her head and let out a screech.

'You mustn't worry, my dear, I'm not going to torture you. I'm sure you know nothing that would be of any interest to me. I just hope your priest calls me before we have to put it to the test.' Sommer walked over to Luigi and took the gag out of his mouth. The young man spat out a tirade of abuse at his captor. Sommer just smiled and whipped the boy across the legs with his walking stick.

'Settle down and tell me why you stole the car?' Sommer barked.

'I will tell you if you let the others go,' Luigi said in Italian. He could barely get the words out with the sweat streaming down his face and into his mouth.

Sommer waited for one of his men to translate and then he shouted: 'You are in no position to bargain.' He whipped Luigi across the legs again. 'Now, tell me why you stole the car.'

'My boss in the Gallico di Palmi crime family—he made me steal it,' Luigi cried.

'What's his name?' Sommer asked when he got the translation.

Luigi kept his mouth shut as he stared into Sommer's eyes. The young Italian let out the faintest of shrieks as Sommer raised his walking stick and cracked him across the jaw with the metal handle.

'Silvio Montagna.'

One of Sommer's men took a note of the name and handed it to a computer technician, who began searching for information on his computer.

'Does he have the missing documents?'

'I don't know what you mean,' Luigi pleaded. 'What missing documents?'

Sommer hit Luigi again with his walking stick and smiled when the young man cried out. He summoned one of his soldiers and shouted his instructions. 'Find this Mafia thug, Silvio Montagna, and bring him to me.' He watched as four of his men climbed into one of the cars and drove off. He turned his attentions back to Luigi, who was crying in pain. 'Do you have the missing documents?'

Luigi looked at his Nazi tormentor but he found no mercy in the man's eyes. 'I swear on my mother's life, I don't know about any documents.'

When he received the translation, Sommer punched Luigi in the face. 'Who has the missing documents?'

The Nazi did not wait for a reply. He realised the young man had fallen unconscious when his eyes closed and his head went limp. He made his way over to a nearby table where Heinrich was preparing electrodes and all manner of ghastly devices designed to dispense electric shocks. 'Revive him,' Sommer ordered.

As a former Stasi operative, Heinrich had no qualms about inflicting pain on their young hostage. However, his experience had told him that further physical cruelty would yield little in the way of meaningful results. The young man was not a trained operative and had already told them everything he knew. Heinrich was more concerned with the fact that his boss had not come to the same conclusion and continued to waste time on the hostages.

In their time together as military unit political officers of the East German State Security Service, Heinrich and Sommer developed a technique of psychological harassment known as *Zersetzung*. The tactics employed involved psychological attacks aimed at destroying the self-confidence of their targets; by damaging their reputation or destroying their personal relationships. Many of the victims thought they were losing their minds, and this often resulted in mental breakdowns and suicide.

In the current circumstances, Heinrich believed they should be focusing their attention on the priest, especially since his father was among the hostages. The priest would bend to their will if the correct amount of psychological harassment were applied. But Heinrich wasn't about to incur Sommer's wrath by making such a suggestion and, even if he did, they didn't have time to wait for the required results. He decided to err on the side of caution by putting his faith in the boss and hoping that he knew what he was doing.

The light in the kitchen seemed to Marcus to be far too bright. He rarely turned on the ceiling light and usually opted for the more subdued wall light. However, in the current circumstances, he realised that ambiance wasn't the main priority. He wondered if perhaps the excessive lighting was part of some draconian interrogation technique. Marcus considered his options as he sat across the kitchen table from Jessica.

Jessica poured herself a cup of coffee and offered Marcus some. 'Look, I haven't been honest with the police,' she admitted.

Marcus sat up, surprised at that revelation.

'I know how to get your father back, but you have to trust me.'

Marcus stared at Jessica and was unsure if he should believe her.

'I work for the British intelligence services—MI6. Her Majesty's government wants the documents that were hidden in the car, but we also want to get those bastards who kidnapped your father. We have technology that will help us find Eamon, technology that is far more advanced than anything the police have.'

'Why haven't you told the police how to get my father back?'

'You have to understand. Our objectives and those of the police are currently aligned, but that might not always be the case. We don't want to share too much with the police. We want to help but we want to do it our way. Besides, they'll fuck it up like they always do.'

'Why should I trust you?'

'You should trust me for the same reason you believe in God—you have faith in a higher power.'

Marcus thought about that for a second and he looked up at Jessica. 'How would those documents help you find my father? From what I could see, they are just the rantings and scribblings of a madman written seventy years ago.'

'So, you admit to finding some documents?'

Marcus didn't answer. He knew the police wouldn't be motivated to find his father until they had a vital piece of the jigsaw. He needed their help but he didn't know who to trust. They needed to know what Marcus knew.

'Okay, okay,' said Marcus. 'I found a journal in the car.'

'What kind of journal?' Jessica could barely subdue her excitement.

'It was written by Rudolf Hess,' Marcus tried to gauge her reaction. 'That's what the Nazis are looking for, I suppose.' Marcus felt confident about revealing the existence of the journal as long as he kept Hitler's letter back as insurance. At least until he knew what was written on it.

'Now we're getting somewhere,' said Jessica. 'Where is the journal now?'

'I've hidden it in a safe place.'

'Do you want me to have the police arrest you for obstructing an ongoing inquiry?' Jessica sounded irritated.

Marcus wasn't so easily frightened. 'Look, your goal is to catch the bad guys, mine is to ensure the safe return of my father, Maria and Luigi. I'm keeping the journal safe until we're ready to call those bastards.'

Marcus looked out the window as Jessica sipped more coffee.

'Look, we need the documents to lead us to these Germans,' Jessica pleaded again. 'We can't call the number they gave us unless we have something to trade.'

'I hid it in a safe place.'

'Where?'

'I will fetch it when we contact the Nazis. No offense, but I don't trust the British. They have occupied my homeland for eight hundred years, all but killing our language and planting so many Scottish Protestants that we will never see the reunification of Ireland in my lifetime. As far as I'm concerned, the English sense of fair play doesn't extend far beyond cricket. So, if it's all the same to you, I think we'll leave them out of this.'

Jessica looked at her watch and frowned as Mancuso returned to the kitchen.

'There's no point in doing any more tonight,' Mancuso said. 'It's late and we're not thinking clearly.'

Marcus rose from his seat and confronted Mancuso. 'We can't wait any longer, they're torturing my father and the others as we speak. We have to do this now—gimme the phone number.'

'Steady on there, Marcus,' Mancuso suggested. 'We can't do this now—we have procedures to follow and laws to uphold.'

'To hell with your procedures—I'm calling the number and sorting this out once and for all.' Marcus stormed out of the kitchen and aimed for the bedroom where Sommer's phone number was scrawled. Mancuso followed him just in time to warn one of his officers to obstruct Marcus's path to the bedroom. Marcus tried to push the police officer out of the way but he was too heavy. Marcus fell to the floor at the police officer's feet.

'The forensics guys will be here a while longer, Marcus. We've arranged for you to stay at a hotel near Interpol's National Central Bureau. Let's get a good night's sleep and meet first thing in the morning to plan our next move. I'll have a guard posted outside your room in case you get any ideas.'

Sommer watched with excitement as Heinrich placed electrodes on various parts of Luigi's body. The electrodes were attached to wires that were connected to the mains. As Sommer stepped closer to Luigi, Heinrich stood to attention and awaited further instructions.

'Please tell me where the documents are hidden,' Sommer pleaded, waiting for the translator to relay the request.

Luigi knew what was coming but he gave the only answer he could. 'I don't know.'

Without waiting for orders from his boss, Heinrich pushed a button on the machine in front of him. Sommer watched as the electricity surged through Luigi's defenceless body. 'Perhaps this has jogged your memory.'

'I swear to all that's holy, I don't know about any documents,' Luigi paused a moment while the translator relayed the information. 'I stole the car on the orders of Silvio Montagna, capo of the Gallico di Palmi family. You can find him in Cisterna di Latina, not far from here. That's all I know.'

Sommer moved closer to Luigi and looked deep into his eyes. 'I believe he is telling the truth, Heinrich.' Sommer thought about that for a moment and considered what to do next. 'So, the Mafia stole the car for no other reason than to sell it off. They had no idea about the documents. That means the priest must have the answers I seek.' He looked at Luigi again. 'But why hasn't he called me to arrange a trade?' He looked over at Eamon. 'Maybe he doesn't believe I will kill you, after all.'

Day Four

10

MARCUS had attained a position of such authority in the Church that only two people had the right to speak to him as if he were an errant schoolboy and get away with it. One of them was addressing him under the dome-shaped ceiling of the Vatican Observatory at Castel Gandolfo.

Cardinal Secretary of State Paolo Bertorelli frowned as he peered through the lens of the giant Vatican Advanced Technology Telescope. He had been silent for some time after Marcus had explained every detail of the events of the past few days.

'Why didn't you alert the authorities of the letter the moment you found it?' Bertorelli asked.

'That would have put the lives of the hostages in jeopardy, your Eminence.'

'Now you have placed the standing of the Holy Roman Church in jeopardy.'

'I think that's overstating it a little, Paulo.'

'That's for me to decide, monsignor, not you,' Bertorelli shouted with a veracity that Marcus had not witnessed in some time. He decided to stay silent until the cardinal's legendary temper had subsided.

Except for the giant telescope and the two men, the circular room was empty. Cardinal Bertorelli had taken to visiting the observatory regularly when the Pope was in residence. Apart from offering unparalleled views of the night sky, the observatory also provided a relaxing escape from the bustle of modern life. That was the main reason why Marcus waited until Bertorelli was under the influence of the dome before he told him about the Nazis and the kidnappings.

Once the centre of astrological research, the observatory had not been used by the Vatican's astronomers for years because urban light pollution began to cloud their views. A new division of the observatory had been established for the Vatican astronomers in 1980 in Arizona.

Cardinal Bertorelli looked at Marcus as he climbed down the steps from the giant telescope, which was built by the Vatican Observatory and dedicated in 1993 by Pope Saint John Paul II.

'What if these Nazis come back and attack the Holy Father?'

'That won't happen, your Eminence. Once I hand over the letter in return for the hostages, they won't bother us again.'

'So, you're going to accept the help of the police and this British woman?'

'Of course.'

'Promise me, Marcus. Promise me you're not going to do anything stupid that will antagonise those murdering bastards.'

'I promise, Paulo, as long as you promise me you're not going to tell the Holy Father about this.'

Cardinal Bertorelli sat next to Marcus on a bench under the giant telescope.

'You will be Camerlengo someday, Marcus. What would you do in this situation?'

'I could never hope to attain the wisdom you have accumulated over the years.'

'Your Irish nonsense won't work on me.'

'Just let me hand the documents over to the Nazis and we'll keep the Holy Father out of it,' said Marcus. 'How does that sound?'

'When you first came here, I was apprehensive, to say the least. The Holy Father had entrusted you with enormous responsibility and I did not believe you would prove worthy of his faith.'

Bertorelli looked around the room, as if to check that they were alone, and then he lowered his voice: 'Every time a pope dies, it is up to me to break in not only the new pope but also the people he brings with him. As the years passed, however, you confounded my expectations. You proved yourself to be not only an exemplary priest but also an honourable man. I know you will do the right thing in this case.'

'That's very nice of you to say, Paolo.'

'The Holy Father has been sent back to Rome, as you know,' Bertorelli said. 'The Italian Prime Minister had requested an audience, so we used that as an excuse. The Italian government wants to borrow more money, apparently. We had to tell the Holy Father that one of the guards was killed during a break-in but we told him nothing about Nazis or stolen limousines. We'll have to tell him about the kidnappings sooner rather than later.'

'My father and the others will be home safely by tomorrow, I'm sure of it.'

'Can you do one more thing for me, Marcus?'

'What is it?'

'When all this is over, let me have Hitler's letter for the Vatican Archives. The real one, not the fake.'

Marcus looked at the cardinal and smiled. He said: 'You're the second most powerful person in the Vatican, how can I refuse you?'

'The third most powerful,' the cardinal said, 'you're forgetting about Signora Locatelli.'

Interpol's National Central Bureau in the centre of Rome was like the offices of any large organisation: drab, unfriendly and altogether too bright. Interpol shared the same building with the State Police and the Carabinieri, an arrangement that irritated Mancuso to the point of distraction.

Marcus was sitting in a chair in the commissioner's office, surrounded by Mancuso, Rossi, and several agents and electronics technicians. Beside him sat a technician who was busy working on a machine hooked up to a laptop. Marcus shuffled his feet as another technician fiddled with his laptop and fine-tuned a cable that ran from the laptop to the telephone. He watched as the man ran another cable from the telephone to a machine on the desk. Marcus wasn't good at waiting and sitting down for long periods, especially when his father was in danger. He wished there were something he could do and that he didn't have to rely on the police to help him find the hostages. He looked down at his hands and noticed they were sweating—then he realised how hot he felt.

'What's the Pope like?' Mancuso asked, without warning. 'Is he a nice guy?'

Marcus looked at Mancuso and forced a smile. 'He has his moments.'

'Does he ever go outside on his own, like in disguise? You know, to walk among his people and get in touch with the real world.'

Marcus thought about that for a moment and then he smiled, for real this time. He was reminded of the time his Holiness had insisted on going to the Campo dei Fiori market. They dressed him up in old clothes, gave him a pair of sunglasses and fitted him with a fake moustache. He wandered around the market for hours under the watchful eye of the Swiss Guard. They had to whisk him away in a hurry when one of the vendors recognised him. There was a bit about it in the paper the next day, but the Vatican denied it.

'His Holiness is God's vessel on earth, of course he doesn't go out among his people.'

'That's what I thought,' said Mancuso. 'Too high and mighty to mingle with the unwashed.'

Marcus found himself annoyed by Mancuso's comment. He seldom reacted well when people offered their opinions about the Pope but this wasn't a normal situation.

'Why don't you just concentrate on getting my father back instead of offering unsubstantiated opinions on things you know nothing about? And, by the way, I don't see why we couldn't have done all this last night.'

Marcus didn't bother trying to hide the agitation in his voice. 'There's no telling what condition my father and the others are in.'

'It's not as easy as that,' Mancuso explained. 'We had to get a court order to run the phone tap and we had to borrow the equipment from the Carabinieri. Be patient,

Marcus, these bastards have no intention of harming your friends. It's not in their best interest.'

'I don't see why you need all this equipment,' Marcus barked.

Mancuso walked over to an elderly man in a tweed jacket who was sitting in the corner of the room. 'This is Doctor Federico Rizzi, a professor of psychology at the University of Rome. He will listen to the phone call you are about to make and ascertain the psychological makeup of our kidnapper. This will give us an insight into how best to deal with him.' Mancuso remained silent for a moment to gauge Marcus's reaction. 'Sitting behind Rizzi is Alfredo, a senior Interpol analyst who might also be able to learn something from the phone call. All this equipment you see here is to trace the call to give us an idea of where the son of a bitch is located.'

Marcus stared out the window like a spoiled child who had just had a dressing down from his mother. The technician seated next to the laptop pressed a key on the computer and nodded at Mancuso.

'Okay, let's get the show on the road.' Mancuso sat in a chair on the opposite side of the desk to Marcus and he dialled the number. They waited until they heard the dial tone through the speakers.

Karl Sommer sat at his desk writing in a journal. He slammed his pen on the desk and ripped out the page he had just been writing on, crunching it in his hands. The mobile phone on his desk rang. He nodded at one of his henchmen, who started typing on his laptop. Sommer's technicians knew the police would try to trace the call and they had a few tricks up their sleeve to give them the runaround.

He answered the phone. 'Hello.'

'This is Monsignor Marcus Nee. To whom am I speaking?'

'Ah Marcus, it's wonderful to hear your voice. How nice of you to call. Let me start by introducing myself. My name is Karl Sommer. Do you have the documents I seek?'

'Yes, I have the documents,' Marcus lied. For the first time, Marcus began to doubt the wisdom of sending the Hitler letter to Willie. *What if Sommer realizes the letter is not in the journal and then kills the hostages?*

'I am in possession of your friends. We are having such a wonderful time together. But perhaps it is time for them to return home.'

Everyone in the Interpol office stared at Marcus, who remained silent. The phone tech gestured for him to keep Sommer on the line.

'I want to speak to my father.'

'Why are you wasting time?'

'Let me speak to him.'

'Very well,' Sommer rose from the chair in the lounge area and walked over to where Eamon and the others were tied up. He gestured for one of his men to loosen the gag over Eamon's mouth and then he placed the phone to the Irishman's ear.

'It's a warehouse, Marcus, a big warehouse—' Eamon shouted, before he was punched in the face.

'Deliver the journal and the letter contained within to the car park opposite Trattoria Ricciotti on the Via dei Pescatori. It is on the banks of Lake Albano. Do you know it?'

'Yes.'

'Good. Come alone at one o'clock. If you are followed by any members of Interpol or the Carabinieri or the beautiful MI-6 agent, I will kill your father, Maria and the car thief. Do you understand?'

'Let me speak to Maria.'

'Do you understand my instructions?'

'Yes.'

At the Interpol office, they heard a click as Sommer ended the call. The technician looked at Mancuso and shook his head: 'Not enough time. We don't know where he was calling from. They routed the call through servers all around the world—a real professional job. Without all the extra safeguards they put in place, I could have traced the call in forty-five seconds.'

'What does that mean?' Marcus shouted. 'All this was for nothing?'

'Not exactly,' Doctor Rizzi said.

'What do you mean?' Mancuso asked.

Rizzi sat up straight in his chair and eyed the room over the top of his spectacles. When he was sure he had everyone's attention, he took off his spectacles and began cleaning them. 'I was able to determine that this is an educated man. He spoke English with barely an accent and he pronounced all the Italian words perfectly. This tells me he is well travelled and comfortable with foreign tongues. He knows more about Miss Barkman than we do, which tells me he has considerable resources at his disposal and a lot of money.'

He looked at Rizzi. 'What else did you learn?'

The professor leaned back in his chair and consulted his notes. He said: 'Sommer took the time to learn the name of one of the hostages, Maria, which tells me he has a family. He is a sociopath, to be sure, but even sociopaths sometimes display empathy when there's a close familial bond. He may have been forced to spend a lot of time away from his family, one person in particular, and he feels guilty about that. However, his priority here is to recover the documents to which he refers. That is his number one objective and he will stop at nothing to achieve it, as evidenced by the fact that he was willing to put Mister Nee on the phone.'

Mancuso stood and looked across the room. 'What about you, Alfredo?'

Alfredo, a short man with a pudgy face, consulted his notes and cleared his throat. 'Mister Nee referred to "a big warehouse," which is quite revealing. He believes the warehouse in which he is being held prisoner is larger than the average warehouse, which means it might not be a warehouse at all, but an aircraft hangar. Since our subject is well educated, well financed and highly motivated, we can assume he arrived in Italy on a private jet. We can also assume he had a good idea where to concentrate his search for the documents before he landed. Since Monsignor Nee's father was deemed a valuable hostage, he would have chosen an airport close to Castel Gandolfo.' Alfredo looked at the Marco Polo City Map of Rome on his desk and smiled. 'I believe we should concentrate our search around unused aircraft hangars near Aeroporto di Ciampino.'

'Talk about the proverbial needle in a haystack,' said Marcus.

'We'll send everything we have to search the area, but we have to focus on Plan A,' said Mancuso. 'Are you sure you've got the items Sommer wants, Marcus?'

'Yes, we'll have to make a stop at O'Reilly's pub on the way to the rendezvous point.'

Marcus was more convinced than ever that he had to find a way to slow down the police and make sure they don't get to the rendezvous point until it's too late. Everyone had their own agenda, he realised, and he trusted nobody. All Marcus wanted was to save his father and the other hostages, so he was determined to follow Sommer's instructions to the letter. Marcus hated pulling the wool over Interpol's eyes, especially since they had gone to so much trouble on his behalf, but it had to be done. Mancuso's heavy-handed approach was bound to get someone hurt.

The best time to ditch the police and Jessica was at O'Reilly's pub, he realised. They would have to stop at the pub to pick up the journal and he hoped it wouldn't be too difficult to get rid of all the surveillance devices and sneak out the back door. He had to assume that the police fitted him with an extra bugging device to make sure they didn't lose him. The only way to make sure he was free of bugs and surveillance devices was to get rid of all his clothes and his phone. He tried to remember who was on duty at the pub. He hoped it was Brian, who was the same size as Marcus and owned his own car. Marcus began to perk up as he devised a plan in his head.

Upstairs, in the smoking garden on the roof of the building, a uniformed police officer was smoking a cigarette while enjoying a bird's eye view of Rome. He looked around to make sure nobody was nearby as he spoke on his mobile phone.

'The car park opposite Trattoria Ricciotti, Via dei Pescatori, on the banks of Lake Albano at one o'clock'.

He switched off the phone, took out the SIM card and tossed it over the side of the building.

11

MARCUS stood in the middle of the office as the technicians fitted him with a bulletproof vest. Mancuso and Jessica watched as Rossi fiddled with the Velcro straps at the back of the vest and tightened them as best he could.

'The vest is fitted with a transponder, so if they take him or if the exchange goes badly, we know where he is,' Mancuso explained.

'Is this necessary?' Marcus asked. 'I can barely move in this thing.'

'These guys are nasty bastards,' said Mancuso, 'Better to be safe than sorry.'

Everyone turned their heads when Jessica Barkman barged in through the door and took off her coat.

'MI-6?' Mancuso shouted as he stared at Jessica. 'I thought you said you were a consulate liaison.'

'Look, the important thing is for Monsignor Nee to get the package so he can make the exchange with these bastards. I suggest that I go along with him to the rendezvous point—I can avoid being seen.'

'Not so fast,' said Mancuso. 'This is police business—we'll handle it from here.'

'Shut up, both of you,' Marcus shouted. 'He told me to go alone, so that's what I'm going to do. I can take care of myself without you two.'

'I don't think that's a very good idea,' Mancuso said. 'These guys look like they're highly trained professionals.'

'Which is why I can't take the risk that they'll shoot the hostages.'

'Don't worry. We're trained professionals as well.'

Marcus grimaced when he realised he might as well be talking to the wall. He stood up and walked around the office to see how the vest felt. 'It won't do me much good if they shoot me in the head, I suppose.'

Mancuso held out a sweatshirt for Marcus. 'Here, wear this over the vest.'

Marcus accepted the burgundy sweatshirt and put it on over the vest. He smoothed it out to reveal the words *Detroit Police Department*. Even the most diplomatic of people would have observed that Marcus looked a hideous sight in the full-length black cassock, the burgundy sweatshirt and the bulging bulletproof vest.

'I look like an eejit,' he said, admonishing his reflection in the window. 'I should have picked up a change of clothes when I had the chance.'

'Don't worry, the Nazis don't care how you look,' Mancuso said as he looked at his watch.

'We have dispatched dozens of police units to the area around Aeroporto di Ciampino, so it's only a matter of time before we find their hideout.'

'What about the British Embassy?' Marcus looked at Jessica. 'What are they doing?'

'We have agents on standby, ready to move at a moment's notice,' Jessica said, moving Marcus to one side, away from Mancuso's earshot. 'You're not helping matters by letting the police take the lead on this,' she whispered in Marcus's ear. 'If you could be just a little more forthcoming about the location of your meeting with the kidnappers, I could call in our helicopters and a dozen agents.'

'We better get going,' Mancuso ordered, gesturing for everyone to make their way to the elevator. One by one, Marcus, Rossi and Mancuso filed into the elevator along with two uniformed officers. Just as Jessica was about to join them, Mancuso stretched out his arm.

'Sorry, sweetheart,' Mancuso said, 'police personnel only.'

Jessica frowned and crossed her arms as the elevator door closed.

'Why do you tease her like that?' Rossi asked Mancuso as the elevator made its way down to the parking level. 'Just ask her out and get it over with.'

'Fuck off, Rossi—pardon my French, Monsignor. Why would I want to date a stuck-up English bitch like that?'

'Because you like her,' Rossi giggled.

'My mother has her heart set on me finding a good Italian, Catholic girl,' Mancuso said. 'You must know plenty of those, Marcus. Can you arrange an introduction some time?'

'Come to Mass one morning at San Tommaso and you can have your pick of the merry widows.'

'You don't want to end up with an Italian girl,' said Rossi, 'you'll end up pistol-whipped and fat.'

When they reached the parking level, Marcus, Mancuso, Rossi and the rest of the team exited the lift and piled into a waiting police surveillance van. The technicians who were already in the van to check the equipment made room for the new arrivals. They closed the doors as the van sped away. Everyone sat on seats along the sides of the van as one of the technicians checked the levels on Marcus's tracking device. Mancuso took his gun out and checked the magazine. Marcus looked at him and frowned. 'You expecting trouble?'

'I always expect trouble.'

'I might need one of those, too.'

'Have you forgotten that you are still a person of interest in this case? Just play your cards right and we'll all get out of this alive.' Mancuso leaned back. 'What's so special about O'Reilly's pub? Why did you leave the journal there?'

'I was in the pub when I discovered the contents of the journal,' said Marcus. 'It seemed like a good place to hide it.'

'That fucking journal will be the death of us all.'

'Your French is getting better, detective,' Marcus smiled.

Mancuso took a gun off the top shelf and handed it to Marcus. 'Be careful, this is loaded. Just click the safety and pull the trigger. I advise you to keep your eyes open when you take aim.'

Marcus accepted the gun and placed it in his cassock pocket.

Twenty-five minutes later, the police van stopped outside O'Reilly's pub in Castel Gandolfo. Marcus got out of the van and went inside the pub. He walked up to the counter and caught the eye of the barmaid.

'Orla, is Brian around?'

'I'll get him for you, Father.'

While he waited, Marcus took off his sweatshirt and placed it on the bar counter. He reached in under the bulletproof vest and started unbuttoning his cassock.

'What can I do you for, Father?' Brian asked as he walked out of the office and approached the priest.

Marcus studied the bartender as he approached and smiled. 'What size are you?'

'I dunno. Same size as you, I suppose.'

'Take off your clothes.'

'What?

'I need your clothes. But first, you have to unfasten this vest.'

Marcus turned his back to Brian to give him better access to the back of the vest. Brian unfastened the vest and lifted it above Marcus's head as the priest lifted his arms. He placed the vest on the bar counter next to the sweatshirt. Marcus took off his cassock and stood in front of Brian wearing nothing but his boxer shorts and his shoes.

It was a happy coincidence for Marcus that the staff at O'Reilly's were required to wear uniforms similar to those worn by priests; that is, before the Pope brought back the cassock.

'You want me to get undressed here in the middle of the pub?' said Brian.

'Come on, there's nobody here to see you. I haven't got all day. I need your shirt and trousers.'

Brian unbuttoned his shirt but he didn't look happy about it. As he did that, Marcus leaned over the bar counter. He reached for the cigar box in the whiskey display case, using the foot rest to gain extra height. With the journal in his possession, he relieved the bartender of his shirt and then took off his shoes so he could put on the trousers.

'I don't suppose you're going to tell me what all this is in aid of,' Brian said as he handed Marcus his black trousers.

Marcus didn't feel like explaining the whole sorry story to Brian. It would take too long and require too many follow-up questions. Besides, the truth was too far-fetched for anyone to believe. Knowing Brian's Irish Republican proclivities and his penchant for the melodramatic, Marcus decided a few white lies would be in order. 'The IRA are after me,' Marcus grunted as he put on the trousers.

'What?' Brian became animated and started looking around, as if the pub was full of hidden gunmen. 'Where are they? What did you do?'

'I can't get into it now. If anyone asks for me, tell them you haven't seen me.'

Brian grabbed the burgundy sweatshirt and put in on. 'I'm not wearing that priest's dress in case they mistake me for you.'

'Very wise,' Marcus said as he tucked in the shirt, zipped up the trousers and buckled the belt. He rummaged through the pockets of the cassock for the gun. When he found it, he tucked it inside his belt.

'How do I look?' Marcus asked.

'You still look like a priest.'

Just then, the door at the back of the pub opened and Jessica burst in. She narrowed her eyes to acclimatise to the darkness and waved when she spotted Marcus. 'Come on, we better hurry.'

Marcus flashed Brian a reassuring smile and ran out the back after Jessica.

'Jaysis,' said Brian, 'this is giving me a newfound respect for the priesthood.'

Back in the van, the police watched the beeping signal on the television monitor. More out of boredom than anything else, Mancuso turned up the volume so the beeping sound got louder.

'The stronger the sound, the closer the subject,' one of the tech guys explained.

'You think it was necessary to plant that second tracking bug on the sweatshirt?' Rossi asked.

'What happens if the Nazis grab him?' Mancuso asked. 'How will we find him? Besides, the second tracker is undetectable, it's one of those organic ones that sticks to clothing and dissolves in twenty-four hours—' Mancuso frowned when his phone rang. He looked at the caller ID and smiled. 'Hello princess. Where are you now?'

'Very funny,' Jessica Barkman said. 'I just called to say I'm having a little trouble identifying your Jane Doe. It's a bank holiday weekend in Britain and the Foreign Office is being difficult.'

'Okay, I guess we'll have to wait until Tuesday then.'

'I have a mate in London who might be able to—'

The beeper sound became fainter and fainter, indicating that Marcus had gone out the back of the bar.

'Shit,' Mancuso said as he jumped out the back of the van. He and the other officers ran into the pub and kept going until they reached the back door. They got to the rear of the building and saw Marcus getting into the passenger side of a dark green Range Rover.

Sitting on the driver's side of the car was Jessica, who was holding her phone to her ear and smiling at Mancuso. The detective sergeant put his phone to his ear and frowned.

'You don't mind if I take over from here, do you?' Jessica purred. 'I'll let you know how we get on.'

Mancuso could only stand and watch as Jessica put her foot on the accelerator and guided the Range Rover out of the car park, leaving a cloud of dust as she went.

'Goddammit.'

Mancuso was not best pleased to see Brian standing beside him in the car park wearing his sweatshirt. He grabbed the bartender by the scruff of the neck. 'Take off my fucking shirt.'

'Take it easy,' Brian stammered. 'It wasn't my idea.'

Just then Rossi burst out through the back door of the pub. 'The tires are flat,' he said. 'She's let the air out of all four tires.'

Mancuso pulled the shirt off Brian and gave him a clip on the ear for good measure.

'Goddammit,' Mancuso said as he walked into the pub carrying the sweatshirt. 'Goddammit to hell.'

12

MARCUS looked at Jessica as she steered the car onto Via dei Pescatori. 'You better be right about this.'

'Trust me,' said Jessica, 'the police would just mess everything up. They are required to follow their procedures and do everything by the book. Besides, I'm better trained than they are. How else can you explain why I was able to sneak up on them undetected and slash their tires while you were in the pub?'

When the lake came into view, they veered south along the shore. 'Look, I know it goes against the grain to trick the police like that, but they deserve it. The Nazis would have spotted them for sure; besides, Mancuso is too full of himself.'

'The German told me to go to the rendezvous alone.'

'Don't worry, they won't be looking at me. They'll be focused on the journal.' Jessica sneaked a peek at the journal as it rested on Marcus's lap. 'Do you have the letter?'

'I still don't feel good about this,' Marcus said.

All Marcus wanted to do was free his father, Luigi and Maria. But he knew they were all dispensable as far as Jessica was concerned. He believed she didn't care if she got the hostages killed. Jessica had insinuated herself into the proceedings despite the objections of Mancuso and of Marcus himself. All she wanted was to get her hands on the journal and the Hitler letter. Marcus assumed she would rob him on the spot if she thought he had the letter.

'The letter Hitler wrote to Hess,' said Jessica. 'Do you have it or not?'

Marcus took the gun out of his pocket and pointed it at Jessica. 'I'm sorry about this but I think you should stop the car and get out.'

'Be careful where you point that thing. It might go off.'

'I'm serious,' said Marcus. 'Stop the car and get out.'

Jessica brought the Range Rover to a stop. 'How about if I stay out of sight in the back and you can drive. Anyway, what do you think you'll be able to accomplish against a bunch of highly trained Nazis? If all else fails, I can follow them and find out where they're hiding.'

'And then what?' Marcus asked. 'Send in the British Army with all guns blazing.'

'Nothing so heroic, I'm afraid. My government wants the documents destroyed.'

'That's no good to me. Your involvement will put the lives of my father and my friends in danger,' said Marcus. 'You have to get out. I'll come back and collect you when it's over.'

Jessica opened the door and got out.

'Happy?' she smiled as Marcus opened the door and walked around to the driver's side. 'Don't you realise that the police know where the exchange is taking place. What good does it do to ditch me?'

'You've already made sure the police won't make it on time. And you know as well as I do that Sommer won't make the exchange there. He'll make sure I'm alone and then he'll send me to a secondary location.'

Marcus kept the gun pointed at Jessica as he got into the car and closed the door. He placed the gun on the passenger seat, grabbed the steering wheel with both hands and drove off. He continued to watch her in the rear-view mirror as he negotiated the narrow road and sharp corners.

As he admired the azure serenity of Lake Albano to his left, Marcus considered the absurdity of his situation. He was attempting to rescue hostages from the clutches of a bunch of crazy neo-Nazis using a journal written by Rudolf Hess. He had been involved in a few scrapes in his life but nothing as surreal as this.

In any event, Marcus knew Sommer wouldn't be satisfied with the journal alone. He cursed himself for separating the journal and the Hitler letter. Now that the letter was on its way to Willie, he risked angering Sommer and endangering the lives of the hostages.

It occurred to him that he didn't have a plan and that he was at the mercy of Sommer and his thugs. The gun was no good to him if they were pointing fifty guns at him. He wracked his brain to figure out some way of changing the odds in his favour.

Marcus knew he had to figure out some way of securing the hostages' release before Sommer realized he had been duped. He hoped Sommer's paranoia and penchant for the dramatic would provide him with the opportunity he needed.

As he turned the corner into Via dei Pescatori, Marcus acknowledged that he could do little to give himself an advantage. At least the Hitler letter would give him some extra leverage if the exchange went sour, he thought.

This looks like the place, Marcus thought as he approached a restaurant on the left side of the road. He stopped the Range Rover right outside the Trattoria Ricciotti and had a good look around. *No sign of anyone.* Putting the car into gear, he drove across the road to the car park, got out and walked around.

Marcus was startled when a woman appeared out of nowhere pushing a pram with a baby in it. She tripped and held on to Marcus for balance. He helped her stand and watched as she moved away. Waiting for the woman to turn the corner, he had another look around the car park. Then he heard what sounded like a phone ringing in his pocket. He took it out and answered it.

'I am delighted to see that you are able to follow my instructions,' Sommer said over the phone.

'I'm in the right place,' Marcus said, 'but you don't appear to be here.'

'That's correct. I wanted to make sure you weren't followed. Now, I want you to go to the town of Albano Laziale, about three kilometres from your current location. There's a cathedral there called Duomo di San Pancrazio Martire. Do you know it?'

'Yes.'

'Good. I will wait for you in the car park to make the exchange.'

'I want to speak to my—' Marcus was cut off in mid-sentence when Sommer hung up the phone. He put the phone back into his pocket and got back into the car.

About three hundred metres away on the far side of the road, two of Silvio Montagna's henchmen were sitting in a red Fiat Punto watching Marcus drive away in the Range Rover.

'They're not taking any chances,' said Paulo, the man in the passenger seat.

'We'll just have to keep following them and see where they take us,' said Dominic, the driver. He started the engine and eased the car forward, making sure to keep far enough behind the Range Rover not to be noticed.

Dominic hated driving the Punto, but he knew it was the most appropriate car to use on this occasion. The silver Humvee the boss had purchased the previous week was more his speed, but it didn't blend in with the surroundings. As he kept pace behind the Range Rover, he hoped none of his henchmen or foot soldiers spotted him in the Punto.

When Marcus arrived at the cathedral at Albano Laziale, he could see two silver Mercedes-Benz S-Class saloons sitting in the car park. Standing next to one of the cars was a middle-aged man accompanied by half a dozen skinheads dressed in expensive suits. Marcus stopped the Range Rover about fifty yards from the cars and switched off the engine. One of the skinheads opened the back door of the Mercedes to reveal Eamon, Luigi and Maria. The old man took out his phone and dialled the only number in the contact list.

'Glad you could make it, Monsignor Nee,' Sommer said when Marcus answered his phone. 'As you can see, I have kept my end of the bargain. Now please, walk half way towards us and place the journal on the ground. Then walk back to your car.'

Marcus did as he was told. He looked on as the skinheads took his friends out of the Mercedes. He stood by as Sommer appeared to be issuing instructions to Maria. She walked toward the journal and kept her eyes on Marcus. When she reached the book, she picked it up, turned around and walked back to Sommer. As she was about to place the journal into Sommer's outstretched hands, she slipped and the journal fell to the ground.

Just then, shots rang out from somewhere in the distance.

Two of the skinheads pushed Eamon and Luigi back into the Mercedes as Sommer and his men ran for cover behind the car. Marcus ran towards the Range Rover and tried to figure out where the shooting was coming from. He looked around and saw the Germans returning fire, but they didn't seem to know where the shooting was coming from either. Except for two skinheads who were lying dead on the ground, they all got back into their cars and seemed to be preparing to depart. Marcus panicked when he saw Maria scurrying across the car park, dodging bullets as she went. The two Mercedes containing Sommer and his Nazis stormed off with guns blazing, leaving their fallen comrades behind. Marcus looked at the spot where Maria had dropped the journal. It was gone.

Maria was standing in the middle of the car park unprotected. Without thinking, Marcus rushed towards Maria and tried to shield her from the gunfire. Just as suddenly as it had started, the gunfire ended and the grounds around the ancient cathedral were once again bathed in silence. But the silence didn't last long.

A red Fiat Punto screeched into the car park and stopped inches from where Marcus and Maria were standing. Marcus braced for impact and looked at Maria. 'This doesn't look good, I'll grant you.'

The man in the passenger seat of the Punto got out and opened the back door. He gestured for Marcus and Maria to get in and appeared irritated when they refused. The man, who was at least twice the size of Marcus, scooped Maria up in his arms and tossed her into the back seat. Just as he was about to do the same with Marcus, the priest raised his hands and smiled. 'I've got the idea—no need to carry me.' Deciding that discretion was the better part of valour, he climbed in beside Maria.

13

SOMMER was not pleased about how the events of the day had transpired. He had lost a hostage and two of his men, and all he got in return was Hess's journal. *There's nothing in the journal that would exonerate the Reich Minister; nothing that would prove he was acting on the orders of the Führer.* He cursed himself for allowing the Pope's errand boy to outsmart him and withhold that which he coveted the most: Hitler's letter. Squirming in his seat, he placed the journal on the desk in front of him and wondered who in the world would have the audacity to shoot at him.

His agents and his loyal soldiers had covered every eventuality, he thought. They had been monitoring the police and they were satisfied that the priest had arrived alone at both rendezvous points. Yet, he couldn't figure out who had scuppered the handover, which he had planned to the smallest detail, or how they had found out where the meeting was taking place. He would have to be more careful next time.

At least we still have two hostages left, he reasoned. He looked over at the two men tied up in the middle of the hangar and he smiled with satisfaction.

He stood and walked over to Eamon. Without warning, he punched him in the stomach. When Eamon stopped coughing and spluttering, Sommer walked closer and looked him in the eye.

'What sort of father are you?' Sommer asked Eamon.

'Fuck off.'

'Do you inspire greatness in your son?'

Sommer sat on a stool in front of Eamon and looked around the hangar. 'When I was a boy, I had a German Shepherd named Rolf. He was my best friend. We went everywhere together. He knew what I was feeling before I knew myself. He cheered me up when I was down and he never left my side. One day, when I was seven or eight, my father took me hiking at the foot of the Bavarian Alps. Rolf came along, too. My father wanted to reach a certain point on the trail and be back at our hotel before dark. On the way back that evening, Rolf got tangled up in some barbed wire and hurt his leg. He was forced to walk with three legs and he couldn't move as fast as normal. My father said Rolf was slowing us down and preventing us from accomplishing our objective. I told him I could walk back with Rolf and find my way to the hotel. But my father explained that once we agreed on a plan, we had to stick to it. He took his Luger pistol out of his pocket and shot Rolf in the head.'

Sommer watched to see the look of disgust on Eamon's face.

'I wasn't angry at my father. I understood his motivation.'

'What's your point?' Eamon said.

'I'm like my father in many ways. If your son doesn't believe I will kill him and everyone he loves in order to accomplish my objective, he is very much mistaken.'

Sommer rose from his stool and returned to his desk. He opened the journal and flicked through the pages. He punched the desk with his fist and let out an exasperated scream.

When the phone rang, Marcus was expecting it. But he was unsure how to handle Sommer, sitting as he was in a Fiat Punto with Maria and a couple of nasty-looking Mafiosi. He could see that they were heading south in the general direction of Valletri Cisterna di Latina. He decided his abduction had something to do with Luigi and that bloody car, but he couldn't help but consider the timing to be unfortunate in the extreme.

'Go ahead, answer it,' said the man in the front passenger seat. Put it on speaker so we can all hear.'

Marcus took the phone out of his pocket and pressed the answer button.

'Our meeting did not go as I had intended,' Sommer said over the phone.

'That wasn't my fault,' Marcus said. 'I don't know who those fellas were. I followed your instructions to the letter.'

'You still seem to have something that belongs to me.'

'What's that?'

'Why do you insist on antagonizing me? I hold your life in my hands and the lives of your friends. Is the letter safe?'

'You'll get the letter when you release my friends.'

'I'm afraid it's not that simple. Since our little exchange didn't go as planned, we'll have to be a little more creative next time.'

'You double-crossed me,' said Marcus. 'You had no intention of releasing the hostages even when you got the journal.'

'You double-crossed me as well by not placing the letter inside the journal.'

'You didn't know that when you drove off with the hostages. I was simply holding onto the letter until I was sure the hostages would be released.'

'I fear you may need more motivation. I am about to kill one of the remaining hostages. The next time I call, you better be more cooperative.'

Marcus played the conversation over in his head when Sommer hung up the phone. *That didn't sound good*, he thought. *Which one of the hostages is the evil bastard planning to kill?* He put the phone back in his pocket and turned to the man in the front passenger seat. 'Where are you taking us?'

'Just relax and enjoy the scenery. My name is Paulo and I have been instructed to take you to my boss, Signore Montagna.'

'Oh, you mean The Mountain?' said Marcus, much to the amusement of Dominic, the driver.

'He prefers to be called *Signore Montagna*,' Paulo shot a disapproving glance at his sidekick.

'I suppose you can explain to me why you barged in on a private gathering and started shooting at all and sundry,' Marcus said.

'As a matter of fact, I can,' Paulo said. 'But Signore Montagna would prefer to explain it to you himself.'

Marcus looked over at Maria and he could see she had been crying. 'Don't worry, mo croi,' he whispered, placing his hand on her shoulder, 'we'll be finished with this nonsense soon and you'll be home with your mother again. You were very brave to get away from the Germans.'

Marcus took out his phone and gave it to Maria. 'You might as well give her a call to let her know you're safe. But it's best to give her as little information as possible.'

Maria smiled and dialled the number.

Marcus looked out the window as the car slowed down and turned left through a gateway that was guarded by two armed men. The wrought-iron gate opened in front of them and they proceeded down the long, winding driveway.

The driveway was lined on either side by rows of cypress trees that seemed to watch over the new arrivals like an army of tall and elegant soldiers. Beyond the trees were rolling hills, fruit gardens and olive fields that went on for miles. In the distance, Marcus could see a sprawling white mansion complete with a domed rotunda in the centre that, even from afar, looked like it could do with a lick of paint. On closer inspection, despite its obvious opulence, the elaborate façade seemed run-down: burned-out tractors and old cars were scattered here and there like rusty remnants of a more industrious past; and the grounds around the fruit gardens were littered with rotten fruit and overgrown weeds. Marcus couldn't help but wonder why the new generation of mafia failed to display the wealth and style of their forefathers.

When the Punto came to a halt next to a row of cars at the side of the mansion, Marcus could hear music, the clinking of glasses and the unmistakable noise of people talking. When Marcus and Maria were ordered out of the car, he peered along the side of the house and could see where the noise was coming from. The back garden was awash with colour as old men and women sat at wooden tables eating and drinking; middle-aged groups huddled together speaking in hushed tones and children ran around playing with kites. Marcus watched as Paulo got out of the car and approached the diners. A handsome, grey-haired man rose from his chair as Paolo approached; the two men hugged for a few moments before kissing each other on the cheek.

Despite his many years living among Italians, Marcus couldn't get to grips with all the hugging and kissing between men. He remembered how fascinated he had been in his youth by the glamour and charisma of the Mafia. He had admired the mafia sense of style and their adherence to the *omerta*, a strict code of silence and honour handed down for centuries. They brought order to society and justice to those who were abandoned by the corrupt police. In fact, if it weren't for the constant hugging and the occasional killing, Marcus could see himself drawn to such a life. After all, it wasn't so much different from the priesthood. But this wasn't something he could confide to his brethren— he'd be shipped off to an impoverished parish in darkest Africa quicker than he could say 'Hail Mary'.

He watched as the Mafia boss beckoned him to an empty table. Marcus smiled as he turned toward Maria and gestured for her to wait for him by the car. He approached the Mafia boss and grabbed his outstretched hand, hoping he wouldn't be required to hug him.

'My name is Silvio Montagna. I'm sorry to have brought you here in such unceremonious circumstances, Padre, but it seems our mutual "friends" are not easy to deal with.'

Despite the informality of their surroundings, Montagna was dressed in an expensive black Armani suit with a light blue shirt opened at the collar. Marcus could not help but admire the man's shiny shoes, which he guessed were made by one of the Italian designers. Marcus saw no point in beating around the bush. 'I will help you find the car if you do me a favour in return.' Marcus shifted in his seat. 'Actually, two favours.'

Montagna placed a glass in front of Marcus and filled it with wine. 'This is quite good,' the Mafia boss said, holding up the bottle. 'We make it here on the estate.'

'Our mutual "friends" have your car and they also have my father and one of my students. I will arrange to meet them again to make a trade. When the time comes, I want you to help me deal with the Germans and rescue my father.'

'What do they want from you?'

'That is not your concern,' Marcus said.

'And the other favour?'

Marcus smiled as one of the rampaging children stumbled into an old man who was about to sip his wine. The red wine spilled all over the old man's white shirt and the boy fell at his ancient feet. Marcus turned his head so that he didn't have to witness the old man's inevitable retaliation. He grimaced at the sound of the boy's screams and turned his attention back to the Mafia boss.

'You employ a boy named Luigi Manetti to steal cars,' Marcus said as he drank from the glass. 'In fact, he stole that vintage Mercedes and then he mislaid it.' Marcus waited for the Mafia boss to nod his head. 'I want you to stop employing him and allow him to continue his studies unmolested.'

'And in return for these favours you will tell me the location of my car,' Montagna said.

Marcus nodded as he took another sip of wine.

'I think that can be arranged,' Montagna stood up and gestured to one of his men to escort Marcus back to the car. 'You tell me where to find these Germans and I'll take care of the rest.'

Montagna buttoned his designer suit jacket and grabbed an unopened bottle of wine from the table. He handed it to Marcus. 'Take this for your journey. My men will take you to the local train station and give you a number you can call.'

14

IT WAS close to midnight when Marcus and Maria arrived at Sperlonga's main square on the bus from Fondi. Like most of the other passengers, Marcus was asleep when the bus came to a stop. If it hadn't been for the bus driver shouting out the name of the town, Marcus might have missed the stop altogether. He woke Maria and helped her off the bus before doubling back to pay the fare. The bus driver groaned with impatience as Marcus struggled to fish the proper change out of his pockets. As the curator of the Pope's summer residence, he didn't have much opportunity to handle money and he was out of practice.

The centre of town was deserted when they disembarked and made their way through the dark, cobblestoned streets. They passed a network of small, white-washed buildings clustered in a maze of warren-like streets, some of which were no more than stone staircases leading down to the sea.

Halfway between Rome and Naples, Sperlonga was a busy little medieval town sandwiched between the Tyrrhenian Sea and majestic Mount Magno. Its whitewashed plaster buildings, small archways and opulent square have for centuries made it a popular and picturesque destination for romantic couples.

Marcus could see that Maria was tired and he was glad they didn't have far to go. She had slept on Marcus's shoulder for most of the bus trip from Fondi but she looked dead on her feet. It seemed like days had passed since they were dropped off at the train station at Cisterna di Latina.

Marcus was tired, too. He was tired of ducking and diving, tired of negotiating with one cutthroat after another, but most of all he was tired of worrying about the fate of his father and Luigi. He cursed himself for finding the journal and not having the good sense to leave it back where it belonged. Why couldn't he have left well enough alone? Why didn't he just put Hitler's letter back in the journal and give the Germans what they wanted? If his curiosity hadn't gotten the better of him, his father would be safe now and this whole sorry mess would be forgotten.

'Just one more corner, pet, and we're there,' Marcus promised.

'Do you think we'll ever see Luigi alive again?' Maria asked without warning.

'You mustn't give up hope,' said Marcus. 'He and my father are counting on us not to give up hope.'

'Sommer said he would kill one of them. I believe he will kill Luigi.'

'What makes you think he will kill Luigi?' Marcus hoped she was right but he hated himself for it.

'Because Sommer has already tortured him and received as much information possible. He will kill Luigi and torture your father next. He knows you will never do what he wants if he kills your father.'

'Jesus Christ, Maria.'

'Before all this happened, I barely considered Luigi. The thoughts I have about him now are confusing. I know I don't love him but I still don't want him to die. Someone will die and I'd rather it be him because he did bad things in his life. Does that make me evil?'

Marcus looked at Maria and considered her dilemma.

'When I was a young man, we were poor,' Marcus said. 'I had an opportunity to go away and get a good education but my father didn't have the money for my travelling expenses. I thought he didn't care about me and I hated him for it. One day, my mother told me to pack my bags because I was going to a school in the big city. I left without saying goodbye to my father because I assumed he didn't care about me. Years later, after I finished school and became a priest, I asked my mother what happened to the gold pocket watch his grandfather had left him. My father had always worn that pocket watch in my youth and I noticed he no longer wore it. She told me he sold the pocket watch so I could go away to school.'

When they turned right onto Via I Romita, Marcus was glad the streets lights were on.

'I treated him so badly for years because I thought he didn't care about me. At the time, I didn't know he had made such a big sacrifice for me. For the rest of my life, I made sure he knew I loved him. The point is that I allowed myself to hate my father because I thought he did something bad to me, and I shouldn't have done that. I should have given him the benefit of the doubt because I loved him. You shouldn't let Luigi's past diminish your feelings for him. People can surprise you, even when they have done bad things. You mustn't feel bad for choosing one over the other. Sommer is the evil one for forcing us to make those choices in our heads.'

As they turned the next corner on Via Cristoforo Colombo, they encountered a festive atmosphere that was in sharp contrast to the eerie tranquillity of the rest of the town. The street was illuminated by a busy pub and they could hear the unmistakable sound of clinking glasses and tall tales told in high-pitched voices. The street itself was full of Harley-Davidson motorcycles, some of which were creaking under the strain of inebriated bodies. Marcus knew from experience that, even though the pub had its own entrance onto the street, it was part of Willie's hotel. They walked over the threshold of the cozy tavern and glided unnoticed through the pub and out the side door into the reception area. Marcus took a quick look at the reservations book and noted the unoccupied rooms. He picked out a key from the wall of keys behind the desk and grabbed Maria by the arm. 'There's a free room on the first floor. You won't have far to walk.'

They climbed the stairs, two steps at a time, and turned right on the first floor. Marcus stopped outside one of the rooms and opened the door. He switched on the light and made room for Maria to enter. 'Make yourself comfortable, pet. I'll go down and meet Willie and then I'll organise some food for you.' Marcus tried to turn and head for the door, but Maria caught his arm and pulled him back. She hugged him and buried her head in his shoulder to hide the tears.

'Don't worry, Maria. We'll sort out this mess in no time at all.'

She released Marcus from her embrace, wiped the tears from her eyes and tried to smile.

'There you go—feeling better already.'

Marcus walked out the door, making sure to lock it, and ran down the stairs. He crossed the hotel lobby and entered the busy pub. He looked around the pub and noticed for the first time that it was full of leather-clad bikers. He spotted a red-faced man with a perpetual smile on his face. Willie was not difficult to pick out in a crowd, with his bulbous nose and bloodshot eyes. He had a healthy skirting of grey hair that drooped to his shoulders even though the top of his head was quite bald.

Marcus sidled up behind his old friend and whispered in his ear: 'Can you tell me the way to Kilronan?'

Willie Shuttleworth Banks turned around with a giddy smile on his face and, in one deft move, grabbed Marcus in a bear hug. He shouted at the top of his voice. 'You made it, dear boy.'

Marcus stood back to take a better look at his friend and was glad to see he looked healthy and happy. He noted that Willie's hair was the only thing about him that could be described as thinning.

'Good to see you again, old man,' Marcus said as he handed Willie the key to Maria's room. 'I've come with a friend of mine. I hope you don't mind, I've deposited her in Room 102 and told her you'd send up food.'

Willie raised his index finger and tapped it against the tip of his nose with a mischievous smile on his face.

'It's not like that, you randy old goat,' Marcus protested. 'I'm a man of the cloth and she's my housekeeper.'

'You didn't have to bring your housekeeper, we have one of our own,' Willie laughed. 'We'll send up some food,' said Willie, 'she'll be fine.' Willie walked in behind, left instructions for the bartender, and liberated a bottle of Connemara whiskey. He returned to Marcus and grabbed him by the arm. 'Let's adjourn to the office and discuss these horrible Huns.'

Marcus first met Willie more than a decade before on the Aran Islands, where Willie had been working as a palaeontologist. He'd had a theory that prehistoric creatures were buried on the northern tip of the island chain and he went there to find their remains. But after years of digging, he'd been unable to prove his theory. Instead, he'd found a hidden shed containing an old pot-still. When his grant from the British Natural History Museum ran out, he decided to clean up the pot-still and go into business selling poteen.

As Marcus was on the island on a short sabbatical to care for his father and help the ageing parish priest, Willie managed to get him to join his nefarious enterprise. Marcus had been short of the necessary funds to repair the dilapidated church, so he decided to take a chance on the poteen trade. Willie had been too old for most of the physical requirements of bootlegging, so he needed a young Turk like Marcus to do the heavy lifting. Besides, Willie hated cutting and mashing potatoes, and he had no time for horses.

Willie had come down from Oxford sometime in the late sixties and ended up selling 'historical documents' to hippies on Carnaby Street. He had been a dab hand at calligraphy and the techniques of the ancient scribes, so he was able to make money writing old manuscripts and passing them off as genuine letters from historical figures. He used only genuine materials that scribes in the relevant century would have used and he made his own sheets of parchment out of animal hide and quill feather pens that would fool most art appraisers. He once sold a minor duchess a love letter purported to have been written by Queen Elizabeth I to Sir Walter Raleigh. Even though Willie had only finished it the previous afternoon, the duchess paid two hundred pounds for it and said she would present it to Queen Elizabeth II at a forthcoming garden party. He always said his biggest claim to fame was that one of his masterpieces was hanging somewhere in Buckingham Palace.

'Can I see the original?' Marcus asked when the two friends were sitting in the hotel office. Willie reached into the bottom drawer of his bureau and pulled out the Hitler letter.

'It just arrived this evening,' said Willie, who placed it on the desk in front of Marcus. They both stared at the document for several minutes before Willie opened the bottle of whiskey and poured each of them a glass.

'Have you had a chance to translate it?' Marcus inquired.

'Not only that, dear boy,' Willie sipped some of his whiskey, 'I've also been able to put it in a bit more of a historical context.' He put on his glasses, cleared his throat and gargled another mouthful of whiskey. He looked at Marcus and proceeded: 'This is a private correspondence in which Hitler gives Hess a last-minute pep talk before Hess embarks on his solo flight to Scotland. Hitler claims to have received an agreement in principle for peace terms with the British. He stresses that Hess's role, as a trusted envoy, is to look the King's brother in the eye and get a verbal agreement. Hitler voices his concern that he has not heard from their liaison in Britain, the Duke of Hamilton, for some time; however, he does not believe this will affect the negotiations. He tells Hess that only senior members of the SS are aware of his mission and he intends to deny all knowledge of it if it fails. He warns Hess to settle his affairs before he leaves Germany and to burn this letter after he reads it.'

'Obviously, he didn't burn it,' Marcus observed.

'You know what this letter means, dear boy, don't you?' Willie asked.

'What does it mean?'

'It means that King George the Sixth was on the brink of making a pact with the devil before someone, probably Churchill, put a stop to it. It also means that Hess wasn't half as crazy as everyone thought he was.'

'They must have known this was going on for a while. Why was it allowed to proceed to that point?'

'I think I have the answer to that, dear boy,' Willie said, taking a large book entitled *Enigma: The Battle for the Code* from the bookshelf beside him. 'The day before Hess flew off on his peace mission to Scotland, on May 9, 1941, the Royal Navy captured the German submarine U-110 in the North Atlantic with its Enigma cryptography machine and codebooks intact. I believe it was this breakthrough, codenamed "Operation Primrose", that prompted Churchill or whoever was monitoring Hitler's peace overtures to pull the plug on the whole affair.'

Willie shuffled through the book and found the page he was looking for. 'They must have considered this breakthrough so important that they could afford to reject whatever deal Hitler was proposing.'

Willie turned the book around so Marcus could get a better look.

'We can never allow this letter to see the light of day,' Willie warned. 'It casts the British in a bad light because they rejected a peace deal with Hitler that would have saved hundreds and thousands of lives. Neither does it look good that they would have considered making a deal to save the British Empire at the expense of France and the rest of Europe.

Marcus looked at Willie and said: 'I'm not sure saving the blushes of the British Empire is our main objective here.'

'Maybe not, my dear fellow. But it also makes Hitler and Hess out to be men of peace and the Brits to be a bunch of warmongers. It will embarrass the British royal family, which I know you don't care about, but it will also inspire a new generation of neo-Nazi fervour. Even an Irishman like yourself must realise that can't be allowed to happen.'

Marcus stared at the Hitler letter. 'There's not much I can do about that; I need the letter to trade for my father and Luigi. If I don't give it to Sommer, he'll kill them both.'

'Perhaps we need some divine inspiration.'

'We need stronger inspiration than that.' Marcus eyed the bottle of whiskey on Willie's desk.

'Don't worry, I have an idea.'

Marcus grabbed the bottle and poured more whiskey into the two glasses. 'What's that?'

'I'll make a forgery.'

'What are you talking about?'

'A forgery,' Willie sipped his whiskey. 'I'll produce a similar letter in which Hitler forbids Hess from going to Scotland.'

'You think you can pull it off?' Marcus asked.

'Why not—you remember I told you about when I used to write those "historical documents" on Carnaby Street back in the day and sell them off to punters?'

Marcus nodded his head.

'Well, I could do the same here only change the content so it doesn't alter history. We could call it an "apocryphal illusion".'

'What about the SS letters, the ones that look like little lightning strikes? You can't duplicate those with a normal typewriter. Sommer will smell a rat if you don't get them right.'

Willie had another sip of whiskey and smiled at his friend.

'We might be in luck, dear boy. After I received your fax yesterday, I went looking for just the thing. What with its Fascist roots, Italy is a hotbed for Nazi memorabilia. I was browsing through an antique shop and came across several old typewriters. The man assured me one of them was made in Germany before the war and that it has the SS key. It stands to reason because all SS and Nazi offices would have had to use a special typewriter after the runic SS character became an official part of the German alphabet in 1939. I tried not to show too much interest in them at the time because I didn't want him to raise the price through the roof.'

'And that just leaves the paper, which had yellowed with age.'

'I've got that covered, too,' Willie said as he opened a drawer in his bureau. 'Due to my proclivity for forgery, I got into the nasty habit of collecting old paper and aging them.'

He took dozens of sheets of yellowed old paper out of the drawer and showed them to Marcus.

'So, you've got everything you need then,' Marcus said.

'Not quite. I still have to find a swastika stamp for the wax seal, but I'm sure the antique shop will have one lying around somewhere. If not, I can always make one myself.

I'll return to the shop first thing in the morning and collect the typewriter.'

The two men smiled and clinked their whiskey glasses.

Day Five

15

THE air in the aircraft hangar at Aeroporto di Ciampino was heavy with the smell of perspiration and sauerkraut. Eamon squirmed in his chair as beads of sweat rolled down his forehead, stinging his bloodshot eyes. He could feel the blisters and abrasions on his wrists and ankle where the rope cut through his skin. He opened his mouth as one of the skinheads spoon-fed him porridge while Sommer sat nearby.

'He's quite something, your son,' Sommer said under his breath. He was reading from an Interpol dossier containing information on Monsignor Marcus Nee. The file included a picture of Marcus and it listed all his accomplishments, assignments and police reports.

Eamon was too busy manoeuvring his fingers into his back pocket to listen to Sommer—and he was in touching distance of the object of his desire. He managed to stretch his fingers so they would reach deeper into his back pocket. He took a tentative hold of the metal figure the Pope had given him—the Mamluk soldier with outstretched sword— and he eased it out of the pocket.

'All-Ireland and international honours in rowing; multiple university degrees; fluent in several languages; assistant to the Papal Nuncio of Ireland; and the youngest ever Director of the Pontifical Villas of Castel Gandolfo.' His monologue was interrupted when he was approached by one of his soldiers.

'Several police vehicles are in the area,' said the soldier. 'We understand from the police scanners that Interpol has received intelligence that we are hiding somewhere in this vicinity.'

'Keep an eye on them. Let me know if they get close.' Sommer looked at Eamon, who seemed to be smiling. 'I would not look so happy if I were you. If the police find us before we can make a deal with your son, it will not bode well for you. You should pray that your son treats me with more respect the next time I call him.'

'He'll have your guts for garters, I'll tell you that,' Eamon said as he took a firmer hold of the Mamluk soldier. He was staring at Sommer, but he was concentrating on the metal figure in his hand. He struggled to manoeuvre it to the optimum position to cut through his binds. Eamon knew the actual sword on the metal figure was sharp enough to cut through the rope because he'd cut himself while playing with it; he just had to direct it properly. With all the other sounds going on around him, he could just about hear Luigi's whimpering to his left. The boy's hands had been tied together and he was hanging by his arms from the rafters, with his feet dangling a few inches from the ground. His body was covered in lacerations and bruises, and Eamon was worried he wouldn't survive his ordeal.

Sommer turned his attention back to the file. He let out a mighty laugh that momentarily startled everyone. 'I see your son is not averse to the odd bout of skulduggery. It says here he was nearly expelled from Saint Patrick's College in Maynooth for organising a poker school. He was given a reprieve when his mentor, an Archbishop Antonio, offered to allow him to finish his studies at the Irish College in Rome. Evidence was later found that he was using the proceeds to start a soup kitchen for the homeless.'

Eamon was still trying to arrange his fingers so that the sword would cut through the rope. He opened his mouth at regular intervals to accept the food he was being given and he chewed before swallowing. When he got the metal figure into position, he began a steady cutting motion across the rope.

'He was accused of operating an illegal distillery on the grounds of the Irish College when one of the priests got drunk after drinking from a holy-water bottle. They could find no evidence against Marcus, so he was allowed to continue his studies. Archbishop Antonio to the rescue again, I think.'

Eamon scowled as he struggled to eat and cut his binds at the same time. For every bit of the rope he managed to cut, he was slicing just as much into his own arm. He tried to relax and act naturally, but the pain was almost unbearable. His sweat was pouring into the incisions made by the metal figure, causing him even more discomfort.

'He has had quite a meteoric rise through the ranks of the Catholic Church. Archbishop Antonio, or should I say the Pope, must think very highly of him. But there's one thing I don't understand. Why would such a well-regarded priest get mixed up with a car thief like Luigi?'

Eamon didn't bother to answer; in any case, he knew it was a rhetorical question. He managed to remove bits of the rope and he could feel the rest giving way. Knowing that he'd have to wait before he could make the next move, he tried not to show his excitement. He was afraid to do any more cutting in case the rope gave way and fell to the ground or he dropped the metal figure.

'I have to admit, he's no ordinary priest, your son,' Sommer said. 'But is he a coward like the rest of his countrymen?'

Sommer stood and lowered his head so that he was inches from Eamon's face.

'The Irish are a cowardly race, don't you think? You hid under the protective apron of your British oppressors during the war and now you take all the money you can get from a European Union bolstered by German industry. It seems to me a worthless nation of beggars and priests—but then they are one and the same, are they not?'

'Plenty of Irish people fought and died in the fields of France during both wars,' Eamon shouted. 'You think sending six million people to the gas chambers was something to be proud of?'

Sommer looked up at Luigi, who seemed to have stopped whimpering. He poked the boy with his stick and waited for a response. 'I feel you are not long for this world, brave Luigi,' Sommer said, turning to one of his soldiers. 'Take him down and dump him somewhere around Castel Gandolfo. Make sure he's dead first.' He got up and walked to his desk.

Eamon watched as the skinheads grabbed Luigi and cut him down. 'You don't have to do this. Marcus will be more inclined to help you if the boy remains alive.'

Sommer just laughed as his thugs carried Luigi over to one of the Mercedes saloons and threw him into the boot. Four men got into the car before it sped out of the hangar.

The man who had been feeding Eamon rose from his stool and walked over to the makeshift kitchen. Eamon waited a few minutes before he returned his attention to the rope. When the coast was clear, he removed the rope from around his bloody arms and stuffed it under his buttocks so it wouldn't be seen. He looked around and saw that everyone in the hangar was occupied. Nobody seemed interested in watching him anymore.

Over a dozen men had congregated to the side of the hangar, where they were concentrating on assembling the vintage Mercedes back to its former glory. Sommer had declared his attention to take the car back to Germany when his business in Italy was concluded. Another dozen or so men were gathered at the makeshift kitchen eating and talking. More men were scattered about and none of them seemed interested in what Eamon was up to.

Eamon reached for his ankle and started untying the rope. The knot was tight but he managed to use the metal figure to sever the threads. When the knot was cut, he gathered up the rope and got out of his chair. He backed away as quietly as his artificial limb would allow and kept an eye out for Nazis as he went. When he reached the middle of the hangar, he hid in the shadows and watched. All the Nazis were preoccupied and hadn't noticed that he was on the move. He turned around and resumed his course to the rear of the hangar. He couldn't believe his luck as the metal door at the back of the hangar came into view. The Germans hadn't spotted him yet and he knew this was his only chance, so he had to make the most of it. When he reached the metal door, he turned the handle and sighed in disbelief. It was locked. He looked through a gap between the door and the wall and watched as a car drove by. Remembering the one weapon he had at his disposal, he reached into his back pocket and took out the Mamluk soldier.

Years before, when Marcus had taken it upon himself to curtail Eamon's excessive drinking, the old man had sought the services of O'Shaughnessy the locksmith, who taught him how to pick locks. Since Marcus had insisted on locking all alcoholic beverages behind locked doors and cupboards, Eamon had to take matters into his own hands. He spent weeks perfecting the art of picking locks, with O'Shaughnessy's help, and he was glad he was now able to put the skill to good use.

He inserted the outstretched sword into the keyhole and jiggled it until he heard a click. After a quick look around to make sure he wasn't spotted, he opened the door and walked out into the fresh morning air. He closed the door behind him and walked as quickly as his artificial leg would allow.

As best as he could make out, he was in the middle of an industrial estate near an airport. In the distance, he could see airplanes landing and taking off at two-minute intervals. He decided the best way to alert the authorities to his predicament was to break through the wire fencing around the airport and make his way to one of the runways. There were no obvious holes in the fence and he didn't have the tools to cut a new opening, so he was left with the prospect of a long walk along the fence.

He was confident that the farther he walked, the greater the chances that he would encounter either a security official or a hole in the fence. He tried to quicken his pace, but it was not easy with his artificial leg. The walk was made more difficult by the necessity to keep looking over his shoulder for signs of the Germans. Eamon hoped that the longer he spent in open ground, the greater his chances of survival. He didn't want to end up like Luigi and he knew that Sommer was getting more imbalanced by the hour.

The only way to get away from the Germans, he thought, was to climb the fence as soon as possible. It could be hours before he found a gate or a hole in the fence that would allow him to enter airport land and make his way to safety. He looked at the fence and realised it wouldn't be easy to climb. He could see no obvious gaps or flaws in the fence that would allow him to scale it.

Then he spotted two wooden pallets lying on the ground about fifty metres away on the other side of the road. He crossed the road and grabbed one of the pallets. When he got back to the fence, he placed the pallet up against the fence and took the rope out of his pocket. He placed the rope between the slats at the top of the pallet and then tied the pallet to the fence, so that the pallet was hanging on the fence about three metres off the ground.

Using the pallet as a ladder, he climbed it until his head was above the top of the fence. He took off his jacket and placed it over the barbed wire at the top of the fence. He was just about to climb over when he saw a flashing blue light in the corner of his eye.

'*Che fai?*' someone shouted from a distance. '*Che stai facendo?*'

Eamon's Italian wasn't up to answering the question, but he could see the man asking the question wasn't in the mood for a chat. As the two airport security officers got out of their yellow squad car with their guns drawn, Eamon eased himself down onto the ground and waited for the officers to approach him from the other side of the fence. Eamon remained frozen on the spot and waited for the men to open fire. Just then, he heard a car pull up behind him. He turned around and his heart sank when he spotted Heinrich getting out of a silver Mercedes.

'*Mi dispiace,*' Heinrich shouted. '*Mio nonno è molto vecchio. Io porterò a casa.*'

'No,' Eamon pleaded as Heinrich grabbed him by the arm and walked him back to the car. 'You don't understand—this man has kidnapped me. Call the police.'

'I don't think they speak any English, grandfather,' Heinrich said as he opened the door of the car for Eamon. When the German walked around to the driver's side of the car and got behind the wheel, Eamon watched as the airport security guards got back into their car and drove away.

Heinrich pointed at an open gate a few metres away from where Eamon tried to climb the fence. 'If you had walked another few metres, you could have walked through that gate and been home free,' Heinrich said. He laughed at Eamon as he drove back to the hangar.

Willie's studio on the top floor of the hotel was appointed with every convenience required by the 'modern man'. It boasted a fully-stocked fridge, a coffee maker, a widescreen television connected to a computer, where Willie enjoyed his black and white movies, a dart board and an architect's drawing table with backlight. It was the perfect escape from the hustle and bustle of ordinary life.

Willie cleared away the papers on his drawing table and cleaned it from top to bottom. He considered the fact that the only time he ever cleaned his studio was when he was about to embark on a project that required a delicate forgery. He was thankful that such projects were now few and far between. He spread newspapers on top of the workbench, unspooled the typewriter ribbon and spread it across the bench. Opening a jar of fountain pen India ink, he took a medium-sized painting brush and dipped the brush into the ink. When the brush was covered in ink, he moved it across to the ribbon and began painting the ink into it. He spread the ink evenly across the ribbon, making sure to cover every inch of it. When he had finished, he placed the painting brush back into the jar of water and waited for the ink to soak into the layers of the ribbon.

Willie glanced at the full-sized black typewriter that was sitting on his writing desk. He admired the craftsmanship and patience that had gone into building the machine, as evidenced by the words 'Continental Silenta' written across the front in gold lettering. He counted himself lucky to have found such a magnificent piece of history and even more fortunate that he had found one with original ribbon spools that were compatible with regular American typewriter ribbons.

But what made this typewriter so essential to his plan was that it featured the runic SS key used by the Nazis. The man in the antique shop said the typewriter was manufactured by the Wanderer Werke company in Siegmar-Schönau, Germany, during the Third Reich. It was the style of machine used by Hitler's secretaries and in the offices of the top SS officers. He said the company made tens of thousands of typewriters during the Nazi era, but this one was special because it was one of those made with the runic SS key. By depressing the shift key and striking the number "3" key, he said, the typewriter typed SS runes in any desired position among a row of letters. Machines like this were used for filling out documents and writing letters where typing a runic SS character was necessary.

When Willie agreed to buy the typewriter, the man in the antique shop even threw in the swastika stamp for free.

Willie amused himself with the notion that this might be the actual typewriter on which the original Hitler letter was written. He imagined Hitler standing over it as a nervous secretary typed out his nonsensical ramblings.

Willie smiled as he tested the ribbon and found that it was still damp to the touch. But he decided it was dry enough to put back into the machine. He picked up the ribbon spools, which were damper and heavier than they were when he began the operation, and placed them back into the typewriter. When both spools were inserted back in their place, he looked at the ribbon and made sure it was attached properly.

He rubbed his hands together and sat down on the chair in front of the desk. Careful to make sure he had cleaned all the ink from his hands, he opened his desk drawer and took out several sheets of yellowed paper. Using Hitler's original letter as a comparison guide, he chose the sheet of paper he wanted and placed the others back in the drawer. As he closed the drawer, he hoped he would only need to use one piece of paper.

When everything was ready, he placed the sheet of paper into the typewriter, twisted the circular handle to the side, and watched as the paper moved along the nine-inch rubber roller to its final position.

As he typed his own version of Hitler's letter onto the paper, he was surprised at the effortless actions of the keys and the ease with which the mechanism still worked. The hammers that struck the ribbon to produce letters on typing paper were counterweighted to make the action smooth and reduce noise. He admired the typewriter again but couldn't help but wonder what evil directives had been issued using its well-crafted keys.

Willie wasn't surprised that Hitler's letter to Hess had been typed. He had read somewhere that because of his lack of education, Hitler rarely wrote anything down by hand. Whenever he needed to write something, he would dictate it to one of his countless secretaries or a trusted friend.

When Willie finished the letter, he read through it and was pleased to see that he would not have to go through the whole process again. He rolled the paper out of the typewriter and read it again. Satisfied that he had accomplished his objective, he placed the letter on the drawing desk and folded it twice.

When he was finished, he placed the original letter in a plastic folder and put it into his safe, secure in the knowledge that the Nazis would never get their hands on it. He poured himself a glass of Connemara whiskey, drank it to steady his nerves and allowed himself a satisfied smile.

16

WHEN she joined Marcus and Willie for coffee at the hotel's terrace bar, Sarah Shannon looked radiant in a simple sky-blue floral summer pinafore under a white cardigan. 'Sorry I wasn't here to greet you last night.'

'That's alright, love.' Marcus stood and kissed Sarah on both cheeks. He studied her for a moment and wondered how she managed to get younger looking every day. Her blonde hair was tied back with a ribbon that matched the colour of her dress.

'Just one kiss, if you don't mind,' Willie joked.

'I was in Rome for a few days for some last-minute shopping before the big day. I hope your problems with your father will be ironed out before tomorrow. Willie told me some of the details last night.'

'I'm sure they will,' Marcus smiled.

Willie had indeed told Sarah a version of the events that had transpired over the last few days, but he left out the more frightening and dangerous aspects. Sarah was told just enough to explain Marcus's arrival so soon before the wedding and Eamon's absence. Both Marcus and Willie were hoping the matter would be resolved before the wedding so they wouldn't have to tell Sarah the truth.

'The Holy Father asked me to thank you for your kind invitation, but he regrets that he cannot attend,' Marcus said, much to the amusement of the others. 'What about Lucy, is she coming?' He asked, referring to Sarah's daughter.

'She said she was on her way,' said Sarah, 'She's in the middle of a management training course in Ireland that Willie sent her to. We're hoping she'll take over the running of the hotel and give us more free time.'

The terrace restaurant was bustling with activity as the staff prepared for the wedding and reception the following day. Marcus could see that Sarah was preoccupied with the arrangements and he knew this wasn't the time to catch up on old times. She was trying to follow the conversation, but she couldn't keep her eyes off the moving of boxes, the arrangement of tables, the blowing up of balloons and the placement of decorations. Marcus watched as the sun shimmered on Sarah's golden hair. The silk ribbon matched the colour of the Tyrrhenian Sea in the distance. He was glad his childhood sweetheart was marrying his trusted friend, but he also harboured a pang of regret. He looked off into the distance and wondered how everything would have ended up if he had taken a different path so long ago.

To Sarah's right, he could just about make out the far-off island of Ponza as it rested on the horizon. To the left, Marcus's eyes were drawn to an odd-looking building standing alone on an elevated outcrop at the end of the beach. 'What's that, when it's at home?' he asked Willie.

'That, my boy, is Truglia Tower, Sperlonga's most recognisable landmark. In the sixteenth century, the

Spanish built it on Roman remains to serve as a watchtower that would allow them to look out for Saracen invaders.'

'What's it used for now?'

'I don't know. I suppose it would make a good museum or a historic coffee shop of some kind. Why do you ask?'

'No reason, it just looks strange, that's all.'

'On the other side of that outcrop, another beach just as nice as this one here stretches out for a kilometre or two. At the end of that beach is the Grotto of Tiberius, where the ancient Roman emperor is reputed to have had many a romantic interlude.'

'Did you hear about our "romantic interlude" there last week?' Sarah asked Marcus. 'It was cut short when Willie's false teeth fell out of his mouth and over the side of the boat.'

Everyone laughed, except Willie.

Sarah reached over the table to pour more coffee, but the pot was empty. 'Excuse me a minute. I'll just go out and make some more.'

'Let the staff do it, darling,' Willie pleaded.

'They're busy—it'll be quicker if I do it,' she smiled and left the table.

'You're like an old married couple already,' said Marcus.

When Sarah was out of earshot, Willie leaned across and spoke to Marcus in hushed tones. 'What happened to the housekeeper?'

'I sent her back to her mother in Rome,' Marcus explained. 'There was no point in her staying here any longer. How are you getting on with the manuscript?'

'Splendidly, old boy, splendidly,' Willie exclaimed. 'It's one of my finest pieces, even if I do say so myself. I'll have it finished by this evening. You're expecting a call from Jerry, I take it?'

'I hope so,' Marcus frowned. 'He'll want to meet somewhere that suits him but I'm going to have to find a way to tip the scales in my favour for a change.'

'Whenever you're ready, we can go up to my studio and study the new manuscript.'

Willie sat up straight when Sarah returned with the coffee. 'What are you two conspiring about?' Sarah smiled.

'He was wondering if you wanted to spend your honeymoon skiing or mountain climbing,' Marcus lied.

'He knows very well I want to do neither.'

'I'm afraid we'll have to take those coffees to go, my dear,' Willie said. 'I promised Marcus I'd show him the plans for the new house.'

'Okay, don't be late for the dress rehearsal tonight,' Sarah said as she offered her cheeks for both men to kiss.

As Marcus looked around Willie's studio, his attention was drawn to the two cream-coloured manuscripts taped to the drawing desk. They looked identical, except that the words were different. Marcus wandered over and studied both manuscripts.

'This is finished except for the final flourish,' Willie explained, hoping that Marcus would ask what he meant.

'What's the final flourish?'

'Hitler's signature, of course,' Willie said, picking up a white sheet of paper on which he'd practiced hundreds of signatures. 'You see how the signature slants downwards as he gets to the end of his name? I have to get that right or the game is up.'

'You've done well,' Marcus observed. 'Most of these are spot-on.'

'I also have to close the letter with red wax and seal it with the swastika stamp,' Willie sat on the wooden stool in front of the desk. 'Then I have to let it dry and open it again.'

Marcus stood over the table and watched as Willie opened a bottle of ink and laid it down next to the manuscript. 'Do you think we'll get away with it?'

'You said it yourself, this Sommer character has no idea what's in the letter. He's just speculating like the rest of us. When he sees this, he might admit his mistake and go home.'

'Or he might go ballistic and kill everyone,' Marcus predicted. 'What does your version say, anyway?'

'I'm glad you asked me that,' Willie said, putting on his glasses. 'In my letter, Hitler beseeches Hess to stop all this nonsense about a peace treaty with the British. He threatens to have Hess stripped of his rank and court martialled if he hears any more talk of the Duke of Hamilton or Joseph Kennedy or King George or anything else to do with this folly. He warns Hess about the dangers of consuming too much herbal medicine and reminds him that he is forbidden from flying for the duration of the war.'

'Nice touch about the herbal medicine,' Marcus said.

Willie put on a pair of white, cotton gloves and picked up his specially designed calligraphy pen. He dusted it with a cotton cloth and then placed it near his mouth and blew off the remaining dust. Dipping the pen into the ink, he looked at Marcus and smiled. 'Well, here goes nothing.'

Marcus leaned forward and watched as Willie signed the word "Adolf" at the bottom of the manuscript in one fluid motion. Willie dipped the pen in the ink again and wrote the word "Hitler", making sure the last three letters appeared in a downward spiral. Willie rested the pen on the cotton cloth and admired his work. He grabbed a hair dryer from the top shelf and began blowing hot air onto the signature to dry the ink.

They both looked relieved when they compared the fake signature with the real one.

'Splendid, I think,' Willie said. 'What do you think?'

'Splendid.'

'Now comes the part I like the most,' said Willie. He picked up the letter and used his two hands to crumble it into a ball.

'Hey, what are you doing?' Marcus shouted.

'Don't panic, dear boy. Sommer would never believe this was real if it didn't have a wrinkle on it.'

Once he had achieved the desired distressed look, Willie straightened out the letter again and folded it as before. Taking a stick of red wax from the edge of the desk, he used a cigarette lighter to melt the wax and spread it on the paper. He grabbed the swastika stamp and pressed it on the wax while it was still soft and pliable. When he lifted the stamp, he was left with a firm impression of the swastika symbol on the hardened wax. The letter was now sealed, as Hitler's secretary would have done more than 70 years before.

Just as Marcus was about to speak, the phone inside his jacket started ringing. He looked at his watch and then looked at Willie. 'Don't let me stay on longer than forty-four seconds.' He checked his watch again and took out his phone.

'Hello.'

'Good evening?' Sommer said on the other end of the line. 'I hope you are well.'

'Let me speak to my father.' Marcus tried not to sound irritated. He looked at his watch: five seconds.

'Are you near a television?'

'Yes,' Marcus gestured for Willie to switch on the television.

'Turn to RAI Channel 1 and watch the news. I'll stay on the line.'

Marcus grabbed the remote control and switched to the correct channel. He watched as the reporter described how a body had been dumped on the road near Castel Gandolfo. The body belonged to a young man of about twenty who had not yet been named. Marcus continued watching as the cameras filmed the body being loaded into an ambulance. He looked at his watch: twenty-six seconds.

'Is it Luigi?' Marcus asked without emotion.

'Correct,' said Sommer. 'You are getting good at this. Meet me at the last rendezvous point in two hours with the letter or I'll kill your father. We will meet inside the cathedral this time. No funny business.'

'No. I have a better idea. You're holding all the aces and I don't trust you. Why shouldn't I pick the rendezvous point? Truglia Tower in the town of Sperlonga. Let's meet at dawn.'

Marcus waited for what seemed like an age as Sommer mulled his proposal. He decided that if he had any chance of saving his father and getting out of this alive, he had to take control of the negotiations to ensure that Sommer couldn't gain an unfair advantage.

'Very well,' said Sommer. Marcus looked at his watch: forty seconds. He hung up the phone before Sommer's men could trace the call.

'Bloody hell,' Willie exclaimed. 'I'm sorry about Luigi, dear boy?'

'It's my fault he's dead,' said Marcus. 'I'm ashamed to say I even hoped Sommer would choose to kill Luigi instead of my father.'

'It's not your fault at all. It's only natural that you would side with your father over Luigi.'

Marcus sat at the table and buried his face in his hands. 'I underestimated these evil bastards, Willie. I should have handled the situation better and secured the release of the hostages earlier. Maybe I was wrong to reject the assistance of the police.'

'You did the right thing, dear boy. The Nazis are to blame for this, not you.'

Before Marcus could reply, his phone rang again. He looked at the caller ID and frowned. He opened the phone and put it to his ear.

'Hello Marcus,' said Cardinal Secretary of State Paolo Bertorelli. 'The Holy Father has just been informed of the full extent of the situation.'

'How is he taking it, Paulo?'

'Not very well. He is aware that Luigi was one of your employees and that you were teaching him English. I have advised him to place his trust in you. He wants to know what you are doing about it.'

'I have just spoken to Sommer,' said Marcus. 'We will meet tomorrow and end this once and for all. I intend to call Interpol, the mafia and even that bloody MI-6 woman. The more people I call, the more the Nazis will be distracted.'

'I hope you know what you're doing.'

'Don't worry, Paulo. I'll have a plan in place before I meet the bastards.'

'What about Luigi? Do you want me to take care of his remains and contact his mother?'

'That would be most kind of you,' said Marcus. 'I will speak to her as soon as I can.'

Marcus closed the phone and put it back in his pocket. He got up from his chair and looked at Willie. 'Meanwhile, you take care of that manuscript. We'll have such a welcoming reception ready for those Nazis that they'll wish they never heard the name Adolf Hitler.' Marcus made for the door.

'Where are you going?' Willie asked.

'I have to come up with a plan but first I have to visit that funny-looking tower. I'll see you later, old friend.'

17

MARCUS stood on the beach and looked up at Truglia Tower. He could see that the impressive white building could be reached by way of two narrow walkways, one of which ran from the beach level to the side of the outcrop on which the tower stood, and one that originated at the highest hill in the town and went downhill toward the tower. At the centre of the courtyard was a stone stairway that led to a door half-way up the tower. Another door was located on the ground floor at the foot of the stairway, which Marcus could see was slightly ajar. Making his way along the walkway, he aimed for the open door. The roof of the tower was probably flat, he thought, which might allow him to access it from the outside.

When he reached the tower, he opened the door wider and stuck his head inside for a better look. The large room appeared to be empty, except for an assortment of tables and chairs that were arranged in the middle of the room.

'Hello,' he shouted. 'Is there anyone here?'

When he got no reply, he opened the door wider and walked in. The room was dark except for a few beams of light that came in through several small windows halfway up the walls. The light beams appeared to be alive as wisps of dust scattered in their path like ants scrambling for food. At the back of the room was another door and a spiral staircase that appeared to reach up to the roof of the tower. Marcus walked across the room and noticed for the first time several wall hangings that hung from the ceiling. He switched on his flashlight and took a closer look at them. They appeared to be coats of arms, but he didn't recognise any of them. When he reached the back door, he nearly tripped on the tattered corner of a worn rug. He gathered himself and opened the door, which revealed a stone staircase that had been cut into the outcrop and led into the sea. He looked on either side of the door and saw that there was little room to walk around. The rear entrance appeared to afford no access to the beaches on either side, or to the roof above. The only purpose for this door, he thought, was to provide easy access to the sea.

He turned around and walked back inside, careful to close the door behind him. He noticed that part of the floor under the carpet felt and sounded different when he walked on it. He pounded his foot on a portion of the floor near the wall and found that it made a louder sound than the rest of the floor. He pulled away the rug that covered the floor and found a wooden panel, complete with a metal handle and hinges. Using the handle, he lifted the panel and found that it was a small door that appeared to conceal a secret passageway of some sort. The door opened on its hinges to reveal stone steps that descended into darkness. Marcus brushed away the cobwebs, which suggested that the door hadn't been used in some time. He made his way down the steps, using his flashlight to light the way forward. When he reached the bottom, he feared there was nowhere else to go. He reached out with his hands and found another door. He opened it and was taken aback when a gust of wind hit him in the face. He marvelled at the white, sandy beach, which was illuminated by the lights of the seaside shops that lit up the night sky as far as the eye could see. He was pleased to see that the pathway before him led down to the beach where he started. As he looked around, he came up with a plan that would scupper the Nazis once and for all. He closed the door and made his way back up the steps.

When he made it back up to the foot of the spiral staircase, he closed the concealed panel, making sure not to lock it, and covered it with the tattered rug. He looked up at the spiral staircase and started climbing. No doors or barriers were waiting to greet him when he got to the top, just a sharp turn that led to the roof. Marcus walked out into the moonlight and admired the view.

He made his way over to one of the walls and gazed upon Sperlonga as it sprawled out in front of him. The image of Luigi's face haunted him and he felt sick to his stomach when he remembered how he hoped Sommer would kill him instead of his father. Why hadn't he practiced the same advice he had preached to Maria, he thought, and why couldn't he remain compassionate amid all this horror. He vowed to avenge the boy's needless death but he hoped he would live to forgive Sommer for what he had done. He looked around and got his bearings before taking out his phone. He pressed some buttons to navigate to the contacts page and then he dialled the number he wanted.

'Silvio Montagna?' he said when the person on the other end picked up.

'Padre, is that you? the mafia boss answered.

'Yes, do you still want to find your Mercedes limousine?' said Marcus.

'Of course,' said The Mountain.

'Okay, listen.' Marcus looked out onto the Tyrrhenian Sea as he relayed his plan to the mafia boss.

Eamon grabbed hold of the railing as he climbed the steps onto Sommer's Gulfstream. He was followed onto the jet by one of the German operatives, who was holding a gun to his back. Once he was seated, Eamon stretched out his arms to allow one of the other Nazis to open his handcuffs and reattach them to the armrest of his seat.

Eamon turned toward the exit when he heard a commotion at the doorway. He watched as three men struggled to carry a rectangular object along the aisle to the centre of the plane. It looked about the same size and shape as a microwave oven, but Eamon suspected its purpose was more sinister than that. Judging by the care with which the men were carrying the object, he feared it might be a bomb.

By the time the door was closed and everyone had taken their seats, Eamon estimated there were nine Nazis aboard, including Sommer. From his vantage point on the luxury jet, he could see Sommer and Heinrich leaning toward a bank of computers at far the end of the plane.

'There's a small airstrip there,' said Heinrich, pointing at the map on the screen, 'in Via Vadorotto, near Terracina, about 30 minutes from Sperlonga.'

'Herr Oberstleutnant, we have vehicles waiting at the airstrip to take us to Terracina,' said Heinz, one of the computer technicians, 'where we will board a speedboat.'

As the jet began to roll away from its position at Aeroporto di Ciampino, Heinrich followed Sommer to two empty seats in the middle of the jet. 'We have analysed the tower in question and found that our best option is to approach by sea. We can dock at the rear of the tower and enter the building without being seen from the land. This scenario will also ensure a clean extraction.'

Sommer closed his eyes as the jet accelerated along the runway and climbed into the air.

'What is our estimated time of arrival,' Sommer asked.

'We should arrive at the tower by four thirty in the morning, Herr Oberstleutnant. Sunrise is at five forty-three.'

'That doesn't give us very much time,' said Sommer. 'What kind of resistance do you expect us to encounter?'

'The priest has been resourceful, sir. We expect quite a bit of resistance from Interpol. However, we will be the first to reach the tower, so we will hold the perimeter by the time everyone arrives. Interpol is based in Rome and they have fewer resources than we do. With a bit of luck, it will be all over by the time they arrive. If the priest wants his father returned safely, he has little choice but to hand over the document. When he does, we can terminate them all and make a clean extraction.'

Sommer smiled as he looked down at the bomb on the floor. 'And we have a little surprise in store for them while we make good our escape.'

'I have to hand it to you,' said Marcus, admiring the copy of Hitler's letter that Willie had just forged. 'You did a fine job, right down to the final flourish.'

'That's very nice of you to say, dear boy,' Willie replied.

Marcus and Willie were drinking cappuccinos at a pavement table outside Willie's hotel as they waited for Jessica to arrive. Against his better judgement, Marcus decided they needed Jessica's help if they wanted to outsmart the Nazis and secure the safe return of his father. She was a professional spy, after all, and she might have a few tricks up her sleeve that might help them. Marcus realised to his shame that keeping his own council had served neither Luigi nor his father well.

'You should think about taking up this line of work full time,' Marcus said, placing the forged document down on the table.

'I used to be a forger, as you know, back in the hazy sixties. One of mine is hanging in the Queen's private study.'

'Oh yes, I remember now—a love letter for the ages.'

'What a memory you have, dear boy.'

'Is the original safe,' Marcus asked.

'There was no original—I made the whole thing up.'

'No, I mean *our* original.'

'Oh yes, quite safe, dear boy,' Willie said, picking up the document. 'We put a safe in behind that dreadful Caravaggio print in the office. Hitler's letter is in there— safe and sound.'

Willie drank a sip of his coffee. He said: 'When is the off?'

'As you know, Sommer called last night and we arranged to meet him at the tower at sunrise,' Marcus said. 'If we leave in the next half hour, we should be there in plenty of time to position ourselves. I called The Mountain to give ourselves a little insurance. When I went to the tower yesterday, I found a secret passageway under the spiral staircase that leads to the beach. I've arranged for a dozen or so armed mafia soldiers to hide in the secret passageway and provide a nice surprise for the Germans. I also called Interpol and, with any luck, we will have completed our business with our German friends and fled to safety before the shooting begins.'

'I hope we haven't over-egged the pudding, dear boy,' Willie said. 'It's supposed to be a simple exchange, not the Battle of Anzio.'

'Better safe than sorry, I always say,' said Marcus.

'You've pitted three violent groups against each other and placed us right in the middle.'

Marcus was just about to answer when a green Range Rover made its way along the cobblestoned alley and stopped beside them. Jessica parked the car and switched off the engine. Willie grabbed the two large duffel bags that were sitting at their table and was at the back of the car before Jessica got out. She pressed the button to open the back door to allow Willie to place the bags inside. Jessica got out of the car and smiled at Marcus. She was wearing jeans, runners and a leather jacket to protect herself against the morning chill. The alley was narrow and Jessica's car left little room for other traffic, vehicular or otherwise. Cars were usually not allowed to enter the alley but few police officers were around at that hour in the morning.

'You going on holidays?' said Jessica. She looked inside the larger of the two bags and then she stared at Willie.

'Just a little insurance, my dear,' said Willie, offering his hand. 'Homemade incendiary devices, Molotov cocktails, that sort of thing. Willie Shuttleworth Banks at your service.'

'Pleased to meet you, I'm sure,' she said, shaking his hand.

'Since I am the professional, I brought a few items of my own,' Jessica said. 'No need to go off all half-cocked.'

'Now look here, young lady,' Willie objected.

'I take it you haven't told the police about our little outing?' Jessica said, ignoring Willie's outburst. 'We don't want them coming in and getting everyone killed, do we?'

Before Marcus could respond, Jessica approached their table and placed her handbag on the vacant chair. 'I say, I'm dying for the toilet. Do you mind?'

She walked towards the entrance to the empty pub and then turned to Marcus. 'Why don't you get me a nice cool Nastro Azzurro for some Dutch courage?' She turned on her heels and headed for the ladies' room.

'Bloody cheek,' Willie said as he returned to his chair.

'Young people these days,' Marcus laughed. 'No respect for their elders.' Marcus got up from his chair and entered the bar to make the drinks.

He returned with the drinks a few moments later to find Willie fidgeting with Jessica's bag.

'The nerve of the woman,' Willie spat.

'Don't worry, Willie. I must confess, I thought you went a bit overboard on the homemade incendiary devices and Molotov cocktails.'

'I spent a lot of time on those, old chap. They are part of my back-up plan.'

'What back-up plan?'

'I'll tell you later.'

Marcus looked down at the table, removing the menu to get a look underneath. 'Where is the fake,' Marcus inquired. 'What did you do with it?'

'I put it in a safe place, don't worry.'

'You're not going to tell me, are you?'

'I'm sorry Marcus, you have to trust me,' Willie said, turning his head to catch the early morning breeze. 'I put it in the perfect place where nobody will find it and we will be able to produce it at the right moment.'

Marcus was annoyed at his friend for keeping secrets from him but he decided not to force the issue, especially since Jessica had just assaulted his ego. He trusted Willie and had faith that the old man knew how to handle the situation. After all, he involved Willie in this dangerous venture and he had to trust him to steer them in the right direction.

'Don't look now,' Marcus pointed down the street, 'There's a police officer coming this way and he looks worse for wear. He's giving Jessica's car the evil eye.'

'Oh, that'll be Benito,' said Willie, reaching for his wallet. 'He's on his way home after a skinful at his sister's bistro.'

Willie took a ten-euro note out his wallet and folded it into the palm of his hand. He walked over to the car, leaned on the bonnet and waited for Benito to approach. He smiled and greeted the police officer with a hearty handshake. Benito gave Willie a little wink and went on his way.

'You're shameless, do you know that?'

Willie sat back down at the table and sipped his coffee. Marcus allowed the cool breeze to massage his face and he detected a hint of brightness on the horizon.

When Jessica returned from the ladies' room, Marcus handed her a drink.

'Are you nervous,' Jessica asked Marcus.

'Yes.'

'It should go smoothly as long as we do what they say,' she said. We hand over the letter and they hand over your father.'

'Easy for you to say,' Willie said.

'You have the letter, I take it?' Jessica asked.

'Willie says he put it in the perfect place where nobody will find it and we will be able to produce it at the right moment.'

Jessica smiled as she glanced at the two duffel bags in the back of the car. 'The rendezvous point,' she said as she sipped her drink. 'Do you know it well?'

'It's the square-looking tower at the end of the beach down there,' Marcus pointed down the hill. 'I noticed it earlier and thought it would make a good spot. I had a gander last night and am now familiar with the layout.'

Marcus slurped his drink and wiped the excess from his lips. 'A narrow road leads to the front of the tower from the "old town". It's too narrow for vehicles, so everyone will have to walk there. At the front of the tower are two entrances, one on the ground floor and one up a flight of steps leading to the second floor. The tower can also be reached via a narrow stairway that starts at the beach.' Marcus paused for questions.

The streetlights were turning off and the morning was getting cooler. Jessica zipped up her leather jacket as she waited for Marcus to continue.

'The right side of the tower has two or three windows, as does the front side. I discovered a secret entrance under the tower and I've arranged a little surprise for the Germans. We should get there well before them and position ourselves near the secret entrance so we can escape afterward.'

'Won't they have snipers stationed around the tower waiting for us?' Willie asked.

'If the Interpol lads are correct about where the Germans are hiding out, they will have a job to get here before dawn, no matter how fast their cars.'

Marcus grabbed a knife from the cheese tray on the table and rose from his stool. He walked over to the other side of the pub entrance, where a makeshift dartboard had been put on the wall. He threw the knife but it failed to stick and fell on the ground. 'The tower itself is dwarfed by the whitewashed buildings of the "old town", which would make a good vantage point for snipers,' Marcus said.

'They won't have time for that, if we go now,' Willie said.

Marcus picked up the knife and took several steps back from the dartboard. 'I was referring to our snipers.'

He threw the knife again. It failed to stick and again fell to the ground.

'What do you mean, *our* snipers?' Jessica asked.

Marcus picked up the knife yet again. 'I called Silvio Montagna and told him the location of the meeting. I also called Interpol.' Marcus took several steps back and tried to shoot again.

'Oh, for goodness sake,' Jessica said as she got up and relieved Marcus of the knife. 'Do it like this.' She showed Marcus the correct action and then she threw the knife. It stuck on the bullseye, right on the centre of the dartboard.

'Let's go then,' Marcus sighed. 'You just watch my back, okay.'

'Consider the resources of Her Majesty's government at your disposal.'

The three of them climbed into Jessica's car and sped off down the narrow alley toward the beach.

Day Six

18

JESSICA steered the car right onto the beach and kept driving until she reached the elevated outcrop of land and rocks on which Truglia Tower was built. Marcus could see the tower above them and was satisfied that none of the windows were visible from their position. Marcus's eyes followed the contours of the outcrop inland as it rose to meet the whitewashed buildings of "old town". He hoped the Mafia were waiting for them up there and he hoped even more that neither the Nazis nor Interpol arrived before them. The Range Rover stopped right at the foot of the narrow steps that went all the way up to the tower.

Marcus got out of the car and opened the rear door, which Jessica had already unlocked from the inside. He reached in to take two shotguns out of the bag. He handed one to Willie along with a handful of cartridges. He looked at Jessica, who had started snickering.

'What's so funny?'

'Are we going pheasant shooting, Mister Bond?'

She snatched the shotguns from the men and put them back in the bag. Grabbing two Sig Sauer P6 pistols out of the glove compartment of the Range Rover, she handed them to Marcus and Willie.

'You need to bring proper guns and leave those ancient artefacts on the beach,' Jessica said to Willie. 'There's a built-in safety—just use extra pressure on the trigger and release the hammer before you shoot.'

'Should we shoot a few practice rounds?' Willie asked.

'And let them know where we are?' Jessica said. 'I don't think so.'

'Now look here, young lady,' Willie was purple with rage. 'You may be GI Jane around here, but I have some military experience, you know.'

'Guns have changed a bit since your time,' she smiled.

'Come on, Willie,' said Marcus. 'You were in the British Army Catering Corp. Your biggest contribution to the war effort was peeling potatoes.'

Willie was too angry to speak. Fearing a temper tantrum that might disrupt their timely arrival, Marcus put his arm around Willie's shoulder and tried to console him. After a moment of two, Willie regained his composure and looked up at the tower.

'The main road to the tower is over there,' Marcus said. 'It leads to the front door. This is a secondary pathway that leads to a secret entrance at the back.'

'You didn't say anything about a secret entrance at the back,' Jessica barked.

'We won't be using it now,' Marcus replied. 'The secret entrance is for our escape.'

'Do you have the letter Sommer requested?' Jessica asked. 'We might have to make a quick trade to avoid bloodshed.'

'Don't worry,' said Marcus, looking at Willie. 'We have the letter.'

Jessica glanced at the duffel bag and then she looked back at Marcus. They closed the trunk and walked up the steps leading to the side of the tower.

'Do you have anything to add, Willie,' Marcus asked his friend, who hadn't spoken in a while.

'The tower was destroyed twice, in 1611 and in 1623, and it was rebuilt each time,' Willie said. 'It is the best preserved of four watchtowers that once stood sentry over the town.'

'I think we can dispense with the history lesson,' Jessica suggested.

'That was a bit rude,' Marcus whispered to Jessica.

It was tough going because there were no lights and the concrete had given way in places. When they made it to the top, the courtyard around the tower was empty.

'It looks like we're the first to arrive,' Marcus said, turning back to his companions. 'Our best bet is to run over to the front door and see if it's open?'

'No,' Jessica said. 'Let's go around to the back and check the back door. It'll be locked but we should be able to force it.'

They made their way along the wall toward the rear of the tower but they had to keep an eye on the ground in front of them so they wouldn't trip on the weeds and long grass. This part of the path wasn't paved at all because it wasn't really a path. When they reached the rear of the tower, they climbed the wall and approached the back door. Marcus turned the door knob and was surprised when it opened.

'It's a trap, Marcus,' said Willie. 'It's bound to be. This is too easy.'

'We're not in a movie,' Jessica said. 'Sometimes things are just easy.'

Marcus walked in and the others followed close behind. His view of the large room was blocked by the wrought-iron spiral staircase and a supporting pillar. 'I can't see anyone. We should still walk along the wall behind the stairs to be on the safe side.'

'I thought this was supposed to be an exchange, not an ambush,' said Jessica.

'I don't trust Sommer to hold up his end of the bargain so there's no point in taking any chances.'

Jessica nodded. They sneaked along the wall behind the stairwell. Willie closed the door behind him so as not to make any noise.

When they turned the corner at the stairwell, all the lights were switched on and Marcus was staring into the face of Karl Sommer. He jolted backward in shock, stepping on Willie's toes in the process.

'Bloody hell," said Willie, who was still unaware of Sommer's presence. 'Watch where you step, will you?"

'I think we have bigger problems," Marcus said, pointing his pistol at Sommer.

Willie pointed his pistol when he looked up and saw who was standing in front of him.

'Is this the rotter who kidnapped your father," Willie asked.

'We'll do the introductions later, shall we?" said Marcus, who was looking at Sommer. 'Let's see your hands, Sommer."

'Or you'll do what?" said Sommer. 'Shoot me? Go ahead, pull the trigger."

Willie didn't need a second invitation. He shifted his aim down and aimed at Sommer's right foot. He squeezed the trigger. Nothing happened. The clicking sound of the metal hammer falling harmlessly was followed by the sound of

Sommer laughing. Willie checked the safety and he pulled the trigger again. Still nothing.

Sommer continued laughing and pretended to be shot, holding his leg as if a bullet had pierced it. Behind him, Marcus heard the click of a cocked pistol.

'You should have gone with the shotguns after all, Marcus,' Jessica purred.

'Allow me to introduce my sister, Helga,' Sommer said. 'I believe you know her as Jessica.'

Marcus turned around and glared at the woman who he thought was his ally.

'That's right, I'm another Nazi motherfucker here to ruin your day,' she said.

Marcus struggled to contain his anger. He knew there was no point in wasting his energy fighting people with loaded guns. He took the time to look around and survey his surroundings. He could just about make out Eamon tied to a chair in the middle of the room. Several skinheads were milling about but they didn't seem to be paying much attention to anything. Marcus had expected to see more Germans; as long as they had all the guns, it didn't matter whether there were five or five hundred. He looked left and right and wondered what to do next.

'There's no need to resort to such foul language, my dear,' Sommer hissed.

'Forgive me, Karl,' said Helga, reaching out to hug Sommer.

When Marcus and Willie dropped their guns, several skinheads swooped in and frisked them. As they were whisked away, Marcus looked back in disgust at Helga and Sommer.

Brother and sister walked arm-in-arm across the room. The former Stasi enforcer guided his sister to a desk in the corner, where he kept his leather briefcase. Helga noticed a photograph in a silver frame inside the bag that was partly visible. She smiled as she picked up the picture.

'Our father is handsome in this photograph,' she said.

'I suppose he is.' Sommer grabbed the picture and placed it back in the bag.

'Why so angry, Karl? Our life's work is at an end.'

'We don't have the letter yet, my dear sister. Our mission will not be accomplished until I have the letter. It's not on his person, so, where is it?

'It's in the car—in one of those duffel bags. I'm sending one of the soldiers to retrieve it.'

Sommer reached out his hand to receive the keys from his sister. He snapped his fingers and threw the keys to one of the skinheads, who went off to get the bag. Brother and sister watched as Marcus and Willie were tied on chairs that were placed on either side of Eamon. Marcus and Willie were no longer wearing their own clothes; they had been stripped and searched, and given dark-blue overalls.

Sommer walked over to the hostages and stared at Marcus. 'This is quite a family reunion. You are reunited with your father and I am joined by my beautiful sister.'

'Your treacherous sister,' Willie spat.

'True enough,' said Sommer, 'but a joyous occasion nonetheless.' Without waiting for a reply, Sommer turned on his heels and walked away.

'I'm glad you could spare the time to come and rescue me,' Eamon said under his breath.

'No trouble at all, Pop. But I'm afraid we've hit a snag.'

'Yes, I can see that. What do we do now?'

'There's something I forgot to tell you, dear boy,' Willie whispered.

'What's that?'

'I took the liberty of recruiting the motorcycle gang that was staying at my hotel.'

'Recruited them to do what?'

'I thought they might create a handy diversion for Jerry while we rescue Eamon and escape.'

'What kind of diversion?' Marcus asked.

'I thought they could use the Molotov cocktails in the duffel bags. I had arranged to leave the bag in the car so they could retrieve the bombs. They were supposed to use them to cause a diversion.'

'Now who is over-egging the pudding?' Marcus asked.

'I didn't know you had already called the mafia and the police, did I?'

Marcus was about to reply when Heinrich approached and placed a table next to Marcus. He draped a linen cloth on the table and then walked away, leaving the three prisoners alone again.

'I thought it would fool the Nazis into thinking they were outgunned,' Willie said.

'You call this a rescue mission?' Eamon interjected.

'Don't be so ungrateful,' barked Marcus. 'I had better things to do on a Sunday morning.'

'Nice to see you again, Eamon, by the way,' said Willie. 'We'll be out of here in no time. I promise.'

'Let me get this straight,' Marcus whispered. 'Your plan was to arm a group of weekend motorcycle enthusiasts with Molotov cocktails so they could overpower an army of ruthless Nazis.'

'That was just a back-up contingency. Our guns were supposed to have bullets in them, remember.'

'What's the name of the gang? Marcus asked.

'The Napoli branch of the Marauders Motorcycle Club.'

'At least you got here in time to say Mass,' said Eamon.

Heinrich approached with a leather bag. He took various dental and surgical instruments out of the bag and arranged them on the table. Marcus tried to see what was coming out of the bag but his attention was drawn to a kerfuffle in the corner of the room.

19

DETECTIVE Sergeant Mancuso was sitting at his desk talking on the phone when he heard a ruckus in the background. He looked up and saw Rossi running towards him.

'Scotty, we have a problem.'

'Not now, can't you see I'm on the goddamn phone.'

'You have to listen to me.'

Just then, the Primo Capitano of the Carabinieri stormed into the station, followed by two men in suits who looked like they meant business. The chief stared at Mancuso as he and the suits made their way into the captain's office.

'Follow me.'

'I'll call you back,' Mancuso said into the phone before hanging up. He looked at Rossi as he got up out of his chair and entered the Primo Capitano's office. He took a good look at the two men who had joined the captain in his office and he decided they were not police officers.

'These men are from the British intelligence services,' said the police chief. 'They are here to help us with our little Nazi infestation.'

'We already have an MI-6 liaison on the case,' Mancuso explained. 'We're meeting her this morning—we have an operation planned.'

'We've identified your Jane Doe from Tor Bella Monaca,' said the taller of the two intelligence officers.

'Who is she?'

'Jessica Barkman.'

'You Italians do amaze me,' Mancuso barked. 'As soon as someone rolls up with a flashy ID card and a smile, you're ready to hand them the keys to the kingdom. How do we know these two clowns are who they say they are?'

'I can assure you—'

Mancuso interrupted the British agents before they could speak. 'So, now we've got a woman running around here posing as a British agent and you want me to clean up your mess.'

'I'm not sure we're accomplishing what we might by fighting with each other,' said the shorter of the two British agents. 'My name is Brian Hawker and this is my colleague, Jim Roddis. We think we can help you to resolve the situation.'

'I'll leave you to it then,' said the Primo Capitano of the Carabinieri, who snapped his heels and turned towards the door. 'I have other problems to tend to.'

Mancuso offered him a sarcastic Nazi salute as he left.

Hawker cleared his throat and put his briefcase on the desk. He took out reams of papers, photographs and maps, and placed them on the desk. He showed Mancuso a photograph of a pretty woman. Mancuso flinched—it was Jessica.

'This nasty piece of work is Helga Sommer, Erich Sommer's daughter and Karl's sister. She killed Jessica

Barkman, our man in Rome, and has been working for Karl Sommer all along to retrieve Hess's documents.'

Hawker put the picture down and held up a picture of an old man wearing an eye patch.

'This psychopath is Erich Sommer,' he said. 'He was Rudolf Hess's chauffeur and personal bodyguard from 1933 until 1941. But he was more than just a lackey—he was a trained SS officer with total allegiance to the Nazi cause. We believe Hess hid documents in his car that proved he was a legitimate peace envoy sent to Britain with the full support of Hitler.' Hawker put the picture down and looked at Mancuso.

'Sommer was supposed to keep those documents safe but he was arrested by Hitler and then tortured by the Russians before he could do that. He wants the world to believe that the Allies caused the death of millions by ignoring Hess. Not to mention the role the British royal family may or may not have played in all this. If this information ever gets out, we will have a new wave of neo-Nazi fervour and global atrocities that will make 9/11 look like a picnic.'

'So, we're fucked,' Mancuso said. 'Sommer already has the journal.'

'Not necessarily. What part does this priest play in all this?' Roddis asked.

'Monsignor Marcus Nee?' Mancuso asked. 'The Nazis kidnapped his father. The trail went cold for us when the Nazis left the body of the car thief near Castel Gandolfo.'

'We believe the priest has a very important document that Sommer needs—a letter signed by Hitler in which he acknowledges his role in Hess's peace mission to Scotland. We are sure Hess kept it as insurance in case the mission went sour, which it did.'

'And they want to exchange the priest's father for this secret letter,' Mancuso added. 'I spoke with the priest last night. He told me the details of the rendezvous and confirmed the handover is planned for this morning.' Mancuso looked at his watch. 'In fact, we were just about to load the helicopters.'

'We'd like to tag along,' said Roddis. 'The priest must still have Hitler's letter and he still believes Helga is on his side.'

'Do I have any choice in the matter?'

'Not really,' said Hawker. 'What can you tell us about the rendezvous point?'

'It's in a seaside resort town called Sperlonga. I'll tell you the rest in the helicopter,' said Mancuso, who was already on the move. 'Let's go,' Mancuso shouted as he led the others out of the office. 'We can be there in about an hour.'

II

High above the tower on the edge of the 'old town', Guido Donati, president of the Napoli branch of the Marauders Motorcycle Club, and five of his comrades were lying in wait among the rocks. Willie's duffel bag, which they had earlier retrieved from the Range Rover, was resting beside them. They looked down below the tower and watched as one of the skinheads ran down to the beach and started searching the Range Rover. Even though the sun had come up, he used a flashlight to scour every nook and cranny of the vehicle and the adjacent pathways. On the roof, another skinhead was watching for movement below.

'What are we going to do with this bag of goodies, Guido?' asked Fabio, the vice-president of the club. 'Do you know how to start a Molotov cocktail?

Guido looked at him as if he were crazy. 'I'm a motorcycle enthusiast, for fuck sake, not Rambo.' He rummaged through the duffel bag. 'Anyway, I looked it up on the Internet. We just open the bottles, which are full of petrol, and stuff them with rags. Then we light the rags and throw them.'

'That sounds easy enough, Guido.'

The MCC president took the bottles out of the bag and placed them in a line on the ground. 'The pros add pieces of Styrofoam to their Molotovs for the "napalm" effect.'

Guido was an assistant bank manager by trade and wasn't used to violent conflict. Not for the first time that weekend, he regretted offering to help Willie and dragging his comrades into harm's way. He knew he'd have to make the best of a bad situation because it was too late to back out now. His colleagues were so excited about the prospect of throwing bombs at Nazis that he couldn't talk them out of it even if he wanted to. They were so keen to spice up their weekend in Sperlonga that they didn't consider the implications of their actions. But if Guido tried to point out the stupidity of their current situation, he would be accused of cowardice and stripped of the presidency. That meant Fabio would have been elevated to the top position and Guido couldn't live with that.

Guido first met Willie when the Englishman applied for a loan to build an extension on his hotel. Before he could grant the loan, he had to visit Sperlonga to look over the property. He ended up not only granting the loan but also falling in love with Sperlonga and with Willie. Since then, he and the Marauders travelled to Sperlonga three or four times a year and Willie always took good care of them. When Willie was in trouble and asked for his help, he felt he had no choice but to spring the Marauders into action and save the day.

III

'What do you mean you couldn't find anything?' Helga shouted, grabbing the car keys from the hapless soldier. She pushed the skinhead out of the way and went outside to inspect the car. She negotiated the stone steps two at a time and, as she approached the car, the look of worry on her face became more severe. '*Scheisse!*'

'What's the matter?' said Heinrich, who had followed close behind.

She slammed her fists against the car and let out a scream. 'The bag is gone. I don't understand it. They must have double-crossed me.'

'Why would they have done that?' said Heinrich. 'They thought you were a British agent.'

'Yes, but I don't think the priest's friend believed I was British.'

'What was in the bag, apart from the letter?'

'It was full of guns and bombs.'

'You stay here and look for the letter,' Heinrich said. 'The priest would not have come here to bargain without bringing the letter. I will go back and see if he is in a mood to talk. I'll send Hans and some of the other men out to help you find his accomplice. They can't have gone far.'

IV

Back in the tower, Marcus watched Sommer and sensed something bad was about to happen.

Sommer approached with one of his skinheads. 'I'm sorry to break up this family reunion, but we have a little business to discuss. I would very much like you to tell me where the letter is. But you must first tell us how many accomplices you have and what they intend to do with their bag of tricks.'

Marcus looked up, startled by this revelation. He looked at Willie, who gave him a knowing wink. Marcus smiled when he realised the bikers Willie had recruited must have remained true to their word.

'I'm glad you find this amusing. I wonder if you'll find it so funny in a few moments.'

Helga entered through the main door and did not look pleased. She kicked a wooden crate out of her way as she approached Sommer. 'We can't find them, Karl. The other two are still looking. They'll turn up.'

'I don't like loose ends, sis. You had a very simple job and you managed to fuck it up.' Sommer walked up to Marcus and punched him in the face. 'Where is the letter?'

Marcus started snickering. 'You're a walking cliché, you know that? You've been watching too many German war movies.'

Sommer looked even more agitated. 'Where is the letter?'

'I'll give you the letter as soon as I see Willie and my father drive away. The letter is nearby.'

'It couldn't be nearby,' Sommer barked. 'Where nearby? Your bag of bombs is gone and we have searched the car. Heinrich has searched you, so we are sure it's not on your person.'

'Trust me. It's nearby. If you let them go I will give it to you.'

'Stop this nonsense,' Helga shouted. 'Let's just kill them now.'

Sommer raised his arm and slapped his sister in the face with the back of his hand, knocking her to the ground. 'Patience, my dear.' He nodded at Heinrich, who took a gruesome utensil off the table and approached Marcus. The priest looked nervous as Heinrich put the utensil, which looked like dentist's pliers, to his mouth and forced it in. The former Stasi agent manoeuvred the pliers to the front of Marcus's mouth and pressed down.

Marcus screamed in agony as Heinrich took out the dentist tool along with one of Marcus's front teeth. Blood spilled out of the priest's mouth as he whimpered in agony.

'Let me ask you again. Where is the letter?'

The two skinheads who had been outside looking for Marcus's accomplice returned. They gestured to Sommer that they found nothing. Sommer again nodded at Heinrich, who approached Marcus. He manoeuvred the dentist's pliers back into Marcus's mouth.

'Wait,' said Willie.

Sommer smiled as Heinrich pulled back.

'Why don't you ask your sister?' Willie asked.

'What are you talking about?' Marcus inquired.

'Bear with me, dear boy', said Willie. 'How well do you know her, Sommer?'

'What are you talking about?' Sommer was losing his patience.

'Have you always been a dutiful brother?' Willie asked. 'Is there anything she might resent you for?'

Helga walked over to Willie and grabbed him by the hair. 'He's just stalling for time, Karl.'

'I'm going to tell him, Helga. I'm going to tell him your little secret.'

Helga let go of Willie's hair and punched him in the face. She grabbed the dentist's pliers from Heinrich and held them close to Marcus's mouth.

'Look inside her handbag,' Willie shouted. 'She had the letter all along. She was going to kill you and sell the letter to the highest bidder.'

Helga moved the dentist's pliers closer to Marcus's mouth, but Sommer raised his hand to her shoulder and pushed her away.

'Check her handbag, if you don't believe me.'

Helga resumed her attempts to get the pliers into Marcus's mouth.

'Wait.'

'You're not listening to him, Karl?'

'Bring me your handbag,' Sommer shouted.

'Karl?'

'Give it to me.'

Helga put down the pliers and walked over to Sommer. She took the handbag from around her shoulder and gave it to her brother. Sommer opened the bag and laid out the contents on the table. It contained a variety of items: a Walther PPK pistol, lipstick, the fake Jessica Barkman driving license, and three utility bills addressed to Jessica Barkman.

Sommer grabbed the utility bills and took the papers out of the envelopes.

Then he saw it.

Inside one of the envelopes was a stained, cream-coloured letter bearing the broken swastika seal and the signature of Adolf Hitler.

Sommer held up the letter and cried. 'I have fulfilled my sacred duty.' He brought the letter closer to his eyes and studied it. Satisfied that the signature and the seal were real, he let out a mighty roar and began sobbing tears of joy.

'You sly old dog,' Marcus whispered to Willie. 'You knew she was a fraud all along and you planted the letter in her bag.'

'Sorry for being so secretive, dear boy,' Willie whispered back. 'I had to give you the option of plausible deniability. By the way, now would be the perfect time for your mafia friends to come out from under the stairs.'

'I was just thinking the same thing,' said Marcus.

Sommer gazed at his sister and the signs of joy were soon drained from his face. He looked over at his skinheads, who were assembled to watch. 'Grab her. I will deal with her in a moment.' He placed the letter on the table and gazed at it without reading the words. He inserted it in a plastic folder and sealed it. He put the folder in his leather briefcase for safe keeping. He grabbed the Walther PPK that had been in Helga's handbag and walked over to his sister. The two soldiers let her go and backed away as Sommer raised the pistol to her head.

'Don't do it Sommer,' said Marcus. 'The police will deal with her now.'

'I'm sorry, priest. If I believed in God, he would be a vengeful God.'

'I swear, Karl, I don't know how that letter got into my bag. He must have planted it while I wasn't looking. He must have—'

Sommer squeezed the trigger and watched as his only sister fell to the ground.

V

Above the tower, Guido and his five leather-clad comrades were alarmed when they heard the gunshot. It was long past dawn and there was a chill in the air.

'That must be our signal to light the Molotov cocktails.'

'What do we do now, Guido?' Fabio asked.

'We're supposed to be tough bikers, we should go down there and attack them,' said one of the other bikers.

'I'm a Chartered Accountant,' said Fabio. 'I've never been in a fight before.'

'Well, why the hell did you become a Marauder?' Guido asked.

'There's no call to take that tone with me, Guido.'

Guido opened each of the five bottles and rummaged through the assorted rags in the bag. He stuffed a rag in each of the bottles and then handed them out to his men.

'What about me, Guido?' said Fabio.

'Have you got a light?' Guido asked, dismissing the question.

'I don't smoke,' Fabio said as he went through the motions of searching his pockets.

Guido looked up at the rest of the men, who shook their heads in unison.

'What the fuck do we do now?' said Guido.

Before anyone could answer, dozens of men appeared out of nowhere carrying guns. Guido and his men watched as they suddenly became surrounded and blocked on all sides. Guido was just about to object when he came face to face with more than a dozen men wearing designer suits and holding machine guns.

'My name is Silvio Montagna,' said the man at the front. 'Who the fuck are you?'

20

MARCUS looked at Willie and whispered: 'How did you know she wasn't English?'

Willie smiled at his friend. 'She was wearing jeans and runners. An English woman on Her Majesty's secret service would never wear jeans and runners; neither would she say, "I'm dying for the toilet." The correct expression would be, "I require the loo".'

'You took a big chance.'

'Not really, I'll tell thee that for nought,' said Willie, affecting a Yorkshire accent. 'A British spy would never order Nastro Azzurro for some Dutch courage, and especially not at four in the morning. I knew she was a fake as soon as I met her.'

'Well, she fooled me.'

'You didn't think there was something funny about her?'

'Not really.'

'If she was working for Six, chances are she would have had a public-school education. I can't put my finger on it, but her appearance and style just didn't smack of Cheltenham Ladies' College.'

'Bollocks.'

'I can't say I'm surprised, old bean. The English have been pulling the wool over Irish eyes for centuries. You just seem to have a blind spot when it comes to the English. Anyway, I had been worried about where to hide the document and then she thrust her handbag onto my lap. I had a root around when you went for the drinks and found some envelopes with bills. I just folded the document in amongst them and let the game play out.'

Their conversation was interrupted by a fracas near the front door, where Heinrich was hunched over a microwave-sized mechanical object that appeared to be connected to a laptop computer.

'The timer has been set, Herr Oberstleutnant,' said Heinrich. 'We have thirty minutes to get clear.'

Heinrich picked up his radio handset when he heard a crackling voice over the speaker. He pressed the button on the handset and replied. Then he turned to Sommer.

'Our friends are here.' Heinrich watched as one of the skinheads opened the main door.

Marcus and Willie looked on in horror as Guido's Marauders, with their arms held high, walked into the chamber followed by Montagna and a dozen of his men.

'So much for my cunning back-up plan,' said Willie.

'And my equally cunning back-up plan,' said Marcus.

'You two are the worst hostage rescuers I've ever come across,' said Eamon.

The mafia soldiers spread out along the walls of the chamber with their guns in hand as the skinheads grabbed the Marauders and tied them up near the others. They were careful not to step too close to the bomb.

Marcus watched as Sommer approached the mafia boss. The German stretched out his arm and handed Montagna a key.

'Your car is waiting for you at our previous location,' Sommer said. 'As agreed, one of my men will accompany you to the correct airport hangar.'

'Much obliged,' Montagna said as he accepted the key.

The mafia boss looked at Marcus before he turned to the door. He said, 'Sorry, Padre, business is business. I weighed my options and decided to err on the side of evil.' Montagna walked out of the tower, followed by his men. When they had all left, the door was closed by another skinhead.

'I don't know why you look so surprised, priest,' Sommer said. 'Nothing good can come from making a deal with the devil.'

Marcus frowned and turned his head toward Sommer, who was busy packing items into his leather briefcase. He'd been outplayed by a better gambler, but he had one more card left to play.

'Are you happy now?' Marcus shouted at Sommers. 'Is that old letter in your briefcase worth the lives of all those people you killed?'

Sommer stopped what he was doing and looked at Marcus. 'With this old letter, I shall rewrite history.'

'We have to go, Herr Oberstleutnant, the speedboat is waiting,' Heinrich shouted. 'We can't wait any longer.'

Most of Sommer's men had already made their way out the back door. They had formed an orderly line and were filing into the speedboat, which was waiting at a concealed location behind the tower.

'You killed poor Luigi, who never hurt a fly. Then you killed your own sister over that letter; doesn't that mean anything to you?' Marcus said.

'She performed her duty as she was trained to do,' Sommer said. 'She betrayed me and our father. I would have let her live if she hadn't double-crossed us.'

'Christmas in the Sommer household must have been a hoot,' Eamon said as he took the metal figure of the Mamluk soldier with outstretched sword out of his back pocket. He used his fingers to manipulate the sword to where he wanted it, and then he began cutting the rope that was binding his hands. He had plenty of practice over the past twenty-four hours, so he was getting good at it.

'She didn't double-cross you at all,' said Marcus.

Willie stared at Marcus. 'Steady on, old chap. He'll kill us for sure if you carry on like that.'

'It's time to leave, Herr Oberstleutnant,' Heinrich shouted again. 'Our snipers have left their position on the roof and the police are approaching. We're sitting ducks.'

'I found the letter in her handbag, where you said I would find it,' Sommer said to Marcus.

'That's because Willie put it there. She didn't even know it was there.'

Marcus and Willie watched as the expression on Sommer's face changed from anger to shame. Heinrich grabbed his boss by the arm and tried to move him toward the back door. Instead, Sommer slumped into his chair and stared at the dead woman lying on the ground in front of him.

'To hell with you,' Heinrich said, turning away from his master and running for the back door.

Having cut through a significant portion of the rope, Eamon took a firm hold of the metal soldier and tried to pry the rope apart with his hands. The threads started to give way and soon his hands were free. Once again, he stuffed the rope under his buttocks so it wouldn't be seen.

'You don't even know what the letter says, do you?' Marcus said.

'What do you mean?' Sommer looked toward his prisoners.

'You were too busy to read the letter. You don't even know what it says.'

'I know what it says.' Sommer took the letter out of the briefcase. He reached for the glasses hanging around his neck and put them on. Placing the letter on the desk, he began to read.

A moment later, he put the letter down and took off his glasses. 'This can't be right. It's just not possible.'

He looked around as the sound of helicopters filled the air and lights flashed through the window.

'It's very possible,' said Marcus. 'The Führer betrayed your father's master. He made a mockery of everything you believe in.'

Marcus was relieved to hear the helicopters outside, especially since his arrangement with the mafia had backfired. This would have been the perfect time for them to emerge from the basement as instructed and overpower Sommer. But they made another deal behind his back. He was even more pleased when he felt the clammy hands of his father cutting through the rope binding his wrists. He didn't know how Eamon managed to be so resourceful but he wasn't about to look a gift horse in the mouth.

'This is not possible,' said Sommer, who grabbed the gun on his desk and approached Marcus.

The priest winced as Sommer shoved the barrel of the gun right up to his head. Marcus fidgeted with the ropes binding his wrists to gauge his father's progress. The rope was looser, but he still couldn't free his wrists.

'What is this trickery, priest? What have you done with the real letter?'

'Why don't you just face the facts and accept that Hess was a madman—and your father was just as crazy.'

'I know what will make you talk.' Sommer grabbed a length of rope off the floor. While keeping a firm hold of one end of the rope, he threw the rest of it over the beam above his head. He caught hold of the other end and started tying a hangman's noose.

Just then, an explosion rocked the front wall, blowing the main door across the room. Sommer was catapulted half-way across the room, along with Marcus, Willie and most of the Marauders, who were still tied to their chairs. Eamon, who had broken free of his chair, landed not far from Sommer. When the dust settled, a large hole appeared where the door used to be. The bomb was still ticking away and seemed to be unaffected by the explosion.

Outside in the courtyard, Mancuso, Rossi and over a dozen Interpol and British intelligence agents looked toward the gap in the wall where the door used to be. They eased forward and tried to see what was going on inside. Mancuso gave the signal to cease fire and watched as the man with the rocket-propelled grenade launcher over his shoulder relaxed his posture.

'Who were those men we saw running away when we landed?'

'I believe those were Silvio Montagna's men,' said Rossi.

'The Mountain? What the fuck were they doing here?'

'They must have been helping the Germans,' said Rossi.

'Sommer must still be inside,' said Mancuso. 'He wasn't in the speedboat with the rest of the Germans.'

Mancuso eased forward and suddenly noticed the rectangular object near the doorway.

'It's a bomb,' said Rossi. 'We better hang back, Scotty.'

Inside the tower, Marcus looked around and saw that Sommer had been knocked to the ground. He tried to free his wrists again and this time he managed to wriggle them loose. Before he could act, Eamon lurched forward and jumped on Sommer, who was still holding the pistol in his hand. Eamon and Sommer wrestled on the floor, causing Sommer to drop the pistol. Before Sommer could react, Marcus manoeuvred himself forward and grabbed the gun.

'It's all over Sommer,' said Marcus. 'Let him go before I shoot you.'

'Stay calm, son,' said Eamon. 'Remember your Romans 12:22—be not overcome of evil but overcome evil with good.'

'Point taken,' said Marcus. 'But Paul's father wasn't being held with a knife to his throat.'

Sommer looked around for support, but he was all alone. The last of his Nazi army had already escaped through the back exit. He managed to get the better of Eamon and wriggled out from under him. He produced a hunting knife from his back pocket and placed it under the old man's neck. Sommer somehow rose to his feet, using Eamon as a human shield.

'Not so fast, priest,' Sommer spat. 'Drop the gun or I'll kill him.'

Marcus kept his gun pointed at Sommer as he manoeuvred behind Willie. He reached down to loosen the rope binding Willie's wrists and waited for the Englishman to wriggle free.

'Any ideas, dear boy?' Willie asked.

'Get the hell out of here, the pair of you,' Eamon barked. 'And take those bikers with you.'

'I'm not going to let him use you as a hostage with all them guns outside,' said Marcus.

Sommer tightened his grip on Eamon as he lurched forward toward the middle of the room. One step at a time, Sommer continued his forward motion toward the front door with Marcus backing away step by step.

Marcus couldn't get a clear shot at Sommer and he didn't want to take a chance on hitting his father. He held himself responsible for Luigi's death and he didn't want to be the cause of death of any more innocents.

Willie used his knife to free the six Marauders one by one.

'Sorry about that, Willie,' said Guido. 'They came from nowhere and took us by surprise.'

'You did yourselves proud, chaps,' Willie said as he freed the final Marauder. 'Walk out of that hole over there and keep your hands up so the police don't shoot you. When you get to the police, tell them it's a bomb and to run like hell.'

Willie watched as the bikers walked out through the hole with their hands and their heads held high.

With Marcus matching his every step, Sommer kept hold of Eamon as they continued across the room. They stopped suddenly and Sommer raised his arm to wipe some sweat from his brow. The Nazi kept his eye on Marcus and Willie as he continued his slow march.

'Where do you think you're going, Sommer?' said Marcus. 'Do you think you're getting out of here alive?'

Marcus could only watch as Sommer continued moving, keeping a firm hold of Eamon as he went. Beads of sweat rolled down Sommer's face, stinging his eyes as he struggled to keep control of the situation. Marcus knew that Sommer didn't care whether he lived or died. For that matter, Marcus didn't care either. All he cared about was that Sommer didn't take Eamon and the rest of them with him. He had to figure out a way to get a clean shot at Sommer.

'Are you forgetting your Scripture, priest? What happened to "turn the other cheek".'

'You've missed your chance at absolution, Sommer.'

'Be careful, priest. You don't want to trip and shoot your father by accident.'

Marcus saw that Sommer was now standing under the beam on which he had earlier thrown the rope. He noticed that the rope was still resting on the beam with both sides hanging down, resting near Sommer's feet. Marcus's mind flashed back to the day his father and the Pope played the re-enactment of the Siege of Acre in the Papal Study. Marcus remembered the events of that famous siege very well because it was one of his father's favourite re-enactments.

'Pop, you remember what happened to the Templars, led by Jean Grailly and Otto de Grandson, when they launched a sudden attack against the Hama during the Siege of Acre in 1291?

'I say,' said Willie, 'do you think this is the best time for a history lesson?'

'It's as good a time as any,' said Marcus, who was still looking at his father. 'Do you remember?'

Eamon looked resolute as he stood in front of Sommer with the knife nestled under his neck. He looked down at the rope at his feet. 'Yes, I remember.'

'Well, bear that in mind for the next thirty seconds,' said the priest.

Marcus pointed his gun, took aim and shot Eamon's artificial leg, just below the knee. Sommer dropped his knife and loosened his grip on Eamon as the artificial limb exploded and crashed across the room. Before Sommer could react, Eamon's dead weight allowed him to fall to the floor. He tied one end of the rope around Sommer's ankles, making sure to tied it with a knot, and threw the other end at his son.

Marcus and Willie grabbed the rope and pulled it as hard as they could. With his legs tied together, the German was powerless to defend himself. They watched in amazement as Sommer was upended and his feet began rising toward the ceiling. Eamon took the opportunity to punch Sommer in the face several times for good measure.

When Sommer's head rose to about half a metre above the ground and he was dangling freely in the air, Marcus tied the rope to a nearby support pillar.

Willie kneeled on both knees and kept an eye on Sommer. 'That was a good trick, dear boy. How did Eamon know what to do?

Marcus smiled. 'During the Siege of Acre in 1291, one of the Templars' attacks failed because their horses got their legs tangled in the ropes of the Muslims' tents. I knew it would remind Eamon to tie the rope around Sommer's legs.'

'Aren't we forgetting something?' said Eamon.

'What's that, Pop?'

'There's a fucking bomb set to go off any second now.'

'Jesus Christ,' said Marcus. 'We'll never get across the room and out to safety on time.'

'What about the back door?' said Willie.

Marcus thought about that and frowned. 'There's nothing out there but treacherous rocks. We'd be shredded to pieces before we reached the shore.' Marcus smiled. 'I have an idea.'

He ran to the spiral staircase and pulled up the carpet at the foot of the spiral staircase. He opened the secret door and shouted as loud as he could. 'This way, lads. Quick as you can.'

Eamon and Willie followed Marcus down the stairs and through the door that led to the beach. Just as the bomb went off and the explosion rocked the tower, they jumped into the water on the edge of the beach. They ran across the soft sand and managed to crawl under the Range Rover just before the rocks and debris started falling on the beach.

Day Seven

EPILOGUE

THE guests sat quietly in the Sistine Chapel admiring Michelangelo's magnificent frescoes as they waited for the wedding of Sarah and Willie to begin. It had been agreed that they couldn't hold the event on the roof of Willie's hotel after Truglia Tower had been blown to smithereens by Sommer's bomb. The debris from the blast had scattered far and wide, and no amount of flowers or decorations could bring the terrace restaurant back to its former glory. Not even the splendour of the Tyrrhenian Sea could hide the devastation wreaked by the bomb. The wedding guests, some of whom had travelled great distances to witness the big event, were easily relocated back to Rome after a few phone calls by Marcus.

Willie and Marcus stood on the makeshift altar near the back of the chapel.

Marcus tried his best to calm Willie, who was fidgeting with the flower in his jacket lapel.

'It's a miracle no one was killed,' said Marcus. 'Except Sommer, of course.'

'What about the rest of the neo-Nazis?' said Jim Dykes, an old friend who had come all the way from Ireland to be Willie's best man.

'They were all picked up by the Italian navy before they reached neutral territory.'

'What about Interpol?' Dykes asked. 'Were any of them hurt?'

'The front of the tower suffered extensive damage, but no harm came to anyone who was outside. Interpol arrested "The Mountain" and dozens of his henchmen at his estate this morning.'

'They didn't catch the Marauders, I see,' Willie said as he waved at Guido Donati in the second row.

'The Marauders weren't carrying any weapons, so there was nothing to charge them with.'

'That's a pity,' said Willie. 'A few nights in jail would have done wonders for Guido's street cred.'

Marcus looked around their exalted surroundings and was glad he was able to salvage the wedding. It hadn't been easy to secure the location at such short notice, but he had been able to pull a few strings. The old place was holding up well, he thought, considering the number of tumultuous events that have taken place outside its walls since it was established by Pope Sixtus IV in 1484.

Marcus smiled as he studied the congregation. Most of the guests were unknown to him, of course, but he was pleased to see a smattering of old friends from the Aran Islands. He smiled at Lucy, Sarah's daughter and the maid of honour, who was standing across the aisle from Dykes. He noticed, sitting at the back, Margaret Sheridan, the Kilronan postmistress and part-time church cleaner, and Mattie Dwyer, owner of the village bicycle rental shop. They were now both married, though not to each other.

Marcus smiled when Eamon approached the altar dressed in an immaculate three-piece suit.

'Are we all set?' Eamon asked. 'It's time to get the show on the road.'

'Just one more thing.' Marcus took from his pocket a small box.

He opened the box and took from it an antique gold pocket watch and chain. Attaching the chain onto the middle buttonhole in Eamon's waistcoat, he placed the watch in his waistcoat pocket. 'Now, you're ready.'

Eamon wiped a tear from his eye and caught Willie smiling at him. 'I had something in my eye,' he said, glaring at Willie and turning to walk back up the aisle.

'What did you do with the real letter?' Willie asked, trying his best to appear nonchalant.

'I presented it to the Pope for safe keeping in the Vatican Archives.'

'Did you tell him the whole story?'

'I couldn't lie to the Holy Father,' said Marcus. 'He promised to keep his mouth shut for a bottle of ten-year-old Bushmills.'

'And what about the fake letter and the journal?' Dykes whispered.

'The MI-6 agents confiscated them,' Marcus smiled. 'I didn't disavow them of the notion that the fake Hitler letter was the genuine article. Serves the arrogant bastards right.'

'Her Majesty will be pleased,' Willie joked. 'That's another one of my masterpieces destined to adorn the walls of Buckingham Palace.'

Marcus turned his attention to the door at the end of the chapel, where Father Allman had been waiting in suspended animation. When Allman gave him the nod, Marcus remembered it was the signal that the Pope was ready. Marcus nodded and turned toward the organist, who also caught the signal and started playing 'Here Comes the Bride'. The congregation turned around in unison to watch Sarah and Eamon walk down the aisle, arm in arm.

When everyone's attention was focused on the blushing bride, Pope John Paul III sauntered in and took his place behind the altar.

Marcus was shocked to see the bump in Sarah's stomach. He turned to Willie and smiled. 'You're full of surprises.'

Sarah looked radiant in a traditional white silk gown, which had been altered to accommodate her baby bump, and her blonde hair glowing in the midday sun. Willie looked on in amazement as his bride-to-be glided towards him.

'She always wanted a big wedding with a long dress,' he said, 'and instead she got a long wedding with a big dress.'

The End

ACKNOWLEDGMENTS

Many thanks to Ian Shuttleworth and Sean Frederick Carey for their editorial input.

AUTHOR'S NOTE

Enigma: The Battle for the Code was written by Hugh Sebag-Montefiore and *Marco Polo City Map of Rome* was produced by Marco Polo Travel Publishing.

CONTACT THE AUTHOR

Twitter: Ronan Joyce@ronan_joyce
Facebook: http://facebook.com/ronan.joyce
LinkedIn: linkedin.com/in/ronan-joyce-1352b0144/
Email: ronan.joyce@hotmail.com
Website: ronanjoyce.com

If you enjoyed this, please check out my other books…

HOLLYWOOD HOODLUMS

Adam and Nigel are desperate to rekindle the fame and fortune they enjoyed in the eighties with a hit song they could never replicate. When their friend Archie writes a screenplay about their brief brush with success, they embark on an unorthodox mission to get it made into a movie. Discouraged by the chilly reception they receive in Hollywood, they meet a scheming rogue who concocts a dangerous plan that promises to get them back on the road to stardom. Luckily for Adam and Nigel, love has a way of thwarting even the best-laid plans.

WEEK AT THE NEES' (MARCUS NEE VOL. I)

On a remote Irish island, the peaceful life of a cash-strapped priest is thrown into turmoil with the arrival of two police detectives on the trail of a fugitive bank robber. Father Marcus Nees' unorthodox business ventures begin to unravel when the island is torn apart by ruthless villains hell-bent on finding the stolen loot for themselves. As Marcus struggles to defend his community, he embarks on a treacherous race against time to save his friends and confront his destiny.

PRAISE FOR *WEEK AT THE NEES'*

'Add to all this enough twists, turns and surprises to have Agatha Christie scratching her head and you've got what they call in the trade a genuine pot-boiler. The race to the ending is thrillingly contrived.'
Paul Dorsey (The Nation)

'So, this questionable priest Ronan Joyce has imagined into being might yet become the Aran Islands' answer to Ken Bruen's detective Jack Taylor. Week at the Nees' is a lively story economically told.
Kevin Higgins (Galway Advertiser)

An excerpt from *Week at the Nees'* follows. Please enjoy.

WEEK AT THE NEES'

CHAPTER ONE

MARCUS Nee stood on the edge of the cliff near his farm and watched in silent anticipation as Judas tried in vain to move his bowels. Unaccustomed as he was to seeing the black and white border collie in such a compromising position, Marcus was reluctant to look away. He was glad of the distraction; anything to take his mind off the pile of potatoes waiting for him in the farmyard below.

His companion since childhood, Judas had all the characteristics Marcus recognised in himself: he was disobedient, had a healthy disregard for authority and was allergic to gluten, to the point of constipation. Despite their apparent lack of affection for one another, they were seldom apart. In the years they had been together, Marcus could find no practical use for the brute and considered him more trouble than he was worth. He sighed as the beast suspended his efforts, scurrying off to find a more secluded location to do his business.

'Ah well, better luck next time. I told you not to eat all that bread.'

Marcus turned towards the sea and watched the waves pounding into the rocks below. Raising his chipped ceramic mug to his lips, he took a mouthful of tea and admired the tremendous span of the Atlantic Ocean. In the distance, he spotted Willie's yacht bouncing across the water, its white sails bulging in the wind. Right on schedule, he thought, looking at his watch. He wondered how many bottles of poteen his friend had sold and what news he would bring from the mainland.

He tried to imagine what the view must have been like more than four hundred years before as the Spanish Armada scuttled homeward with its weary sailors throwing cannon and horses overboard as they went. He could almost see the mighty galleons with their tattered sails as they crashed into the Irish coast.

When the wind picked up, Marcus bowed his head to protect his eyes. He turned around and made his way back to the farmyard to finish his work and check on the old man.

It would be a gross understatement to say that Marcus disliked cutting potatoes. But it had to be done—they were the main ingredient in his poteen, and they were cheap and plentiful. There was no getting around the fact that they had to be cut and mashed to facilitate the distilling process. It was the price of doing business and, in the scheme of things, it was a small price to pay. It weighed heavily on his mind that he had to break the law to make the money he needed. He considered some of the other illegal activities he could have pursued and, as nefarious enterprises went, distilling poteen was the safest option. Robbing a bank would take too much planning and there was also the chance he could get shot. Kidnapping a wealthy business tycoon would be too messy, especially considering his disproportionate guilt complex. All things considered, poteen was the best option, even if he disliked the process.

In the distance, he could see his father, Eamon, sitting on a gate, dangling his foot against the rusted metal. Marcus had no idea what the future held for the pair of them, but he hoped it had nothing to do with potatoes. As he neared the stone wall that marked the edge of his farm, Judas appeared out of nowhere and darted between his legs, nearly tripping him. Marcus cursed as he broke into a run and jumped the stone wall. Clearing it with inches to spare, he landed on a mound of soft hay on the other side and was careful not to break his ceramic mug. Standing up, he brushed the hay off his clothes and ran his fingers through his thatch of thick brown hair. He caught himself admiring his reflection in the discarded windscreen of an old tractor. Not bad looking for a man of forty, he thought to himself. His nose and mouth were smaller than normal, but his chin was prominent enough to tie the rest of his face together with a distinguished flourish. In contrast to the rocky fields of Inis Mór, he had an air of congeniality and purpose.

When he reached the middle of the yard, he sat down on the three-legged milking stool and returned to the task at hand.

Cutting potatoes in cold weather was a tricky proposition, as Marcus discovered once when he almost lost his fingers. A decent pair of rubber gloves and a sharp knife were definite requirements. It was also important to make sure the potatoes were clean, so they didn't subvert the distilling process.

Conditions at the farmyard were far from ideal but Marcus had streamlined the process to reduce the amount of heavy lifting involved. To save himself from lugging heavy sacks of potatoes from the kitchen all day, he set up his enterprise in the farmyard so that Shergar could do all the work. Marcus was sure the old nag would have preferred to spend his days frolicking in the fields, and he didn't blame him. But if he wanted to be fed and watered every day, he had to do some work.

Marcus had already been through at least three hundred potatoes and his hands were almost frozen solid. The wind coming in from the Atlantic was as cold as he had ever experienced.

Nearly finished, he promised himself, just a few more to go.

'You better stay on your toes,' Eamon shouted. 'I heard Lucy is back.'

Marcus remained silent, unwilling to involve his father in a topic that had been causing him several sleepless nights lately. He couldn't think about Lucy now—he was struggling to grip the knife with his frigid hands.

'It'll be pissing down soon,' said the old man, shifting on the gate and losing his balance. He righted himself just in time but couldn't prevent his bottle of poteen from landing on a fresh pile of horseshit.

Marcus looked up at the sky and then checked his watch. 'You're joking,' he told his father. 'There isn't a cloud in the sky. Are you making a weather forecast or a philosophical observation?'

Eamon growled as he repositioned himself on his wrought-iron perch. 'Get that bottle for me, will you, like a good man?'

Marcus ignored his father and was annoyed the old man had nothing better to do at that hour of the morning. Just because he was elderly and handicapped didn't mean he could lounge around all day drinking.

'There are eight hundred people who live on this bloody island and you're the only one who doesn't do any work.'

'Can't you see I'm disabled?'

Once a tall, elegant man, Eamon had become withered and scrawny in old age. Even so, he had lost none of his poise and his cold blue eyes seemed to mellow when he smiled. He was proud of the fact that his teeth were his own—though he was missing a few at the front, which allowed him to affect a ghastly sneer when the situation required it. He always wore a tweed cap with a matching jacket and a single wellington boot with the top turned down.

Eamon had lost his right leg in a farm accident a few years previously. He had a perfectly good prosthetic limb, but he preferred not to wear it around the farm, thus underscoring his inability to work.

Marcus looked at his watch again. He was behind schedule—he'd only just finished cutting the spuds. His fingers had had enough, though, so he rose from his stool and rinsed his hands in a bucket of water. He dried them on a towel and put on his warm leather gloves.

'His lordship will be here soon,' said Marcus, walking over to his father. He picked up the bottle of poteen, taking extra care not to get any excrement on his gloves, and handed it to the old man. 'Why don't you make yourself useful and put the kettle on?'

Ever since Eamon's accident, Marcus had had the unenviable tasks of looking after his father and managing the farm. There was a limit to what Eamon could do around the place, but there seemed to be no limit to the damage he could cause, both to himself and to the farm. Marcus didn't mind putting his life on hold to look after the old man. His father raised him after his mother died, so he owed him a great deal.

The old bugger had farmed these fields of useless muck and stones near Cockle Strand for more years than he could remember. And his father before him had done the same. Marcus inherited the land after the old man's accident—or at least he inherited the work. His only saving grace was that he had found a better use for the land than his father and his father before him. He discovered he could make more money using the potatoes to distill illegal poteen than selling them at the market.

'Make your own bloody tea,' Eamon shouted as Marcus climbed over the wall at the end of the yard and untied Shergar. He backed the animal towards a two-wheeled cart that was already loaded with bags of cut potatoes. After a few failed attempts, Marcus managed to raise the cart to the proper height and attach it to the horse's harness. He made sure all the straps were tight, and then he slapped the animal on the rump.

The Nees used to own two horses, but one of them had died mysteriously. Marcus didn't know it for a fact, but he suspected the poor creature had downed some poteen that his drunken father had left in the yard. Now he'd have to get another beast at the Maam Cross Fair—when he could scrape the money together.

'That's all the booze you're getting now, so make it last,' he said to Eamon, who was still sitting on the gate.

One of the measures Marcus had to implement while caring for his father was a restriction on the amount of poteen the old man was allowed to consume. Just because they had a steady supply of the illegal brew didn't mean Eamon could help himself to what he liked. He was allowed half a pint daily for medicinal purposes and the rest was kept under lock and key. The owners of the island's pubs and shops were also under strict instructions not to serve the old man.

As he guided Shergar over to the beach, Marcus allowed himself a smile at the thought of his one-legged father hopping through horseshit to get back to the house.

As Marcus and Judas made their way across the muddy fields to the inlet, he cursed the weather and pulled the lapel of his overcoat up over his ears. At least it's not raining, he thought. Inis Mór was a desolate place during the winter months. The treeless landscape provided hardly any shelter from the savage ocean winds and the barren limestone fields provided little sustenance for the farmers who laboured in appalling conditions.

But it was beautiful, too. The craggy landscape and the sheer cliffs were known throughout the world for their magnificence. The grey-purple sky seemed to intensify the colours of the island, the fields of green and the thatch-roofed cottages of stone.

Marcus loved Inis Mór and he took his duties and commitments seriously. He thrived on the tranquillity and the long summer days when nature was in full bloom. And then there was always the important task of catching up with the latest gossip at the local pub. He lived for the days spent fishing at Serpent Hole, playing Gaelic football on the beach or rowing his currach for hours around the island.

Thanks to his rowing, he was much fitter than would normally be expected of a man of his age. Like most of the islanders, Marcus had learned to row at an early age.

When he studied for his Leaving Certificate with the Jesuits in Galway, he represented the school at several international regattas. He did the same when he studied at

Trinity College in Dublin. He competed at dozens of currach-rowing festivals around Galway Bay and across the country, including the world-famous Cruinniu na mBad Festival in Kinvara. He still holds the record for being the fastest person to row the thirty-five kilometres from Inis Mór to the mainland.

Marcus raised his head when he reached the inlet and spotted the white sails in the distance. He looked south and could clearly make out the islands of Inis Meáin and Inis Oírr sprawled out across the ocean. Judas barked as he ran ahead of his master towards the shore. Willie's yacht provided a wonderful spectacle, rising and falling over the waves as it neared the beach. Marcus watched as his friend dropped anchor, jumped onto the little jetty and made his way onto the beach.

'How's it going, your lordship?'

William Shuttleworth-Banks wasn't a lord, but Marcus liked to tease him about his posh English accent. Just because they were firm friends didn't mean he could be forgiven for being English.

'Nice weather for it, my boy,' Willie lied, rubbing his hands against the cold.

'So, how's business?' Marcus asked.

'Not bad at all, dear boy.' Willie reached into his pocket to take out a wad of cash. 'Sold the whole lot this trip.'

'Things are picking up then?'

Marcus accepted the notes and smiled. He was curious about the sales aspect of the business, but he knew Willie would never divulge his contacts or say where he sold his poteen.

'At any given time, there's a party going on somewhere in Ireland.' Willie leaned on his yacht and admired the limestone contours of Aran. 'You just have to follow the sound of the music, dear boy.'

Marcus and Willie had built their little poteen business into a lucrative venture. They had only one pot still but the overheads were low and they were making plenty of cash. Marcus grew the potatoes, they distilled the liquor in a shed at the back of Willie's home and they used Willie's yacht to distribute the finished product.

While Marcus knew his friend had recently shown signs of restlessness and suspected he wanted to pack it in, he hadn't considered the consequences of this. The business had been good to them but it wasn't easy money. They had to work hard for their ill-gotten gains and they had plenty of competition. Like any business, they had to keep their customers happy with a quality product and reliable deliveries. But it wasn't a young man's game and Marcus was mindful of the fact that Willie was getting on in years.

Willie grabbed hold of Shergar and guided the spud-laden animal towards the water's edge. He stopped for a moment and placed his hands on his hips, palms down with his thumbs pointing forward, as if to straighten his body to relieve a backache.

'You don't look so good,' said Marcus. 'Are you feeling okay?'

'Just a touch of the gout, dear boy.'

Marcus looked at his friend. 'I heard Lucy was back and trying to cut into our action. Have you bumped into her on your travels?'

'Not yet.'

'She's trying to find our poteen still, I suppose.'

'She'll never find it. My little island is well off the beaten track.'

'If anyone can ferret it out, it'll be her.'

'Speaking of ferrets, how's the old man?' Willie smiled. 'I haven't seen him in a while.'

'Contrary as ever—whatever you do, don't give him any booze.'

'Chance would be a fine thing.'

Marcus began lifting the bags of potatoes into the boat. When the wooden baskets were empty, he turned Shergar around and headed back to the farm to fetch another load.

This had become a twice-monthly routine for the partners. Every second Monday, Willie would moor his yacht near the Nees' farm and pick up the potatoes. When the boat was loaded, Willie would raise anchor and head off to his home at the lighthouse on Rock Island, off the northwest coast of Inis Mór. They would meet up every Wednesday to bottle the poteen in the shed next to Willie's lighthouse and load the bottles onto the boat.

All they had to do was stay friendly with Garda Sergeant Gilligan, a functioning alcoholic who relied on their services as much as anyone. Marcus plied him with poteen every week in exchange for a general amnesty.

This weekly supply of booze to Gilligan also took care of Willie's accommodations at the lighthouse on Rock Island, a protected bird sanctuary that was out of bounds. Nobody bothered him because the island was cut off from Inis Mór on its north western tip and shielded from view by Brannock Island, which was located between the two. Whenever ornithologists turned up to study the local cuckoos, swallows or house martins, Willie would disrobe and dance around naked like a deranged hippy—that was enough to rid him not only of the ornithologists but also the birds.

Marcus liked the bootlegging routine and he enjoyed being entertained by Willie at his lighthouse. The old white tower had been abandoned for years but Willie had made the effort to return it to its former glory. It was full of books, objets d'art and oddities he had picked up during a lifetime of travelling the world. Marcus liked browsing through the library and he enjoyed the wonderful dishes Willie prepared when the work was done for the day. They would sometimes take Willie's boat to Kilmurvey or Kilronan and spend the night sampling the whiskies at Ivor's Pub before Marcus headed home through the fields.

It was the perfect set-up.

When Marcus and Shergar returned to the beach with another load of potatoes, Marcus held out the reins for Willie. 'Can you take it from here, your lordship? I'm late for Mass.'

Willie took the reins with a mischievous grin. 'Fair enough. Say a prayer for me.'

'I don't have that kind of time.' Marcus knew his old friend was a devout atheist and he suspected his soul was beyond redemption. They both laughed as Marcus looked off in the direction of Kilronan. 'What are you up to for the rest of the day?'

'Not much,' Willie said. 'I'm off to Galway tonight to do a bit of business. I'll be back on Wednesday for the bottling.'

'Is there anything wrong?'

'Nothing to worry about, old chap. I just have a few loose ends to tie up.'

Marcus waited for more information but all he could do was watch as Willie guided Shergar back up the hill towards the farm. He'd accepted that his friend was secretive and understood it was just a by-product of the poteen trade. It didn't do to have loose lips in the illegal alcohol business. If

Willie had something to say, he would say it when he was ready.

It started raining when Marcus turned around and began his journey across the beach towards Kilronan.